Seeker of Justice

A Detective Hardwick Novel

B.J. Woster

Thank you to the editors at Global Bookworms for their part in editing this work (https://www.globalbookreviews.net/)

Contents

Dedication

To my daughters, without whom this book would never have been written. Thank you for your love and support throughout the years. I love you all dearly.

Prologue

Sometimes when life hands you lemons…well that's all you get. Sure, you can make the lemonade, but without sweetener, that drink will give you one hell of a sour punch. What's the sweetener? In life, that's different for everyone. For me, it was the smooth stretches along my rather rutted, perilous road. But I got to where I am now and I'm still standing…most days. My daughter recently exclaimed, after one of my youthful anecdotes, "Geez, Mom, don't you have any happy stories?" I do, of course, but there's something about trauma that sears into your brain making it easier to overshadow the good memories.

My childhood was like most. Put a ball within reach and I'd hit it, kick it, or throw it. Put me near a tree and I'd climb it. Storm drains nearby? You better believe I was shimmying through one, until I discovered, quite rapidly, that I was claustrophobic. That put an end to the storm drain adventures. I was a tomboy through and through. I loved to run and so I ran everywhere. Even competed in running in school. The 100-meter dash was my specialty, and I won the medals to prove I was pretty daggum fast.

Yep, my childhood was average until around the age of thirteen, then everything started to go to Hell in a handbasket. It was about this time when life started teaching me lessons that no thirteen-year-old should need to learn. No, not the kind of lessons your brain probably leapt to—those lessons started a few years later—but you probably weren't far off the mark, as it was in my pubescence that I discovered just how evil people could be. Did they make me evil? No, nor will I resort to the 'devil made me do it' stance, as I was perfectly capable of making my own decisions without influence of a malevolent entity. Still, I could say the actions of others drove me and there is truth in that, for had the actions of others not silenced me so thoroughly, I may not have elected the outlet that I did to be heard.

I won't drag you down my memory rabbit hole for too long before getting to the crux of my story, but it is an important element in mental development. After all, for one to comprehend another's mind, you must step inside that mind. Wouldn't you agree? One thing I will divulge—I learned I'm capable of murder…but aren't we all.

~ Seeker of Justice

Chapter one

Bethany lay beside her husband, who snored louder than the train whistle that blew unfailingly, infuriatingly, at four a.m. as it rumbled along the tracks alongside Whitehall Street. Her home, on Lillian Avenue, sat on a small plot several miles from the rails, but the distance didn't prevent the piercing sound drifting into their bedroom and disturbing their much-needed rest. She glanced over at Shane, still sawing logs and realized that it was only *her* much-needed rest that was disturbed night-after-night—by Shane's snoring, when he wasn't at work, and that damnable train whistle. She rubbed her eyes and wondered how much longer she'd have the will to live. Of course, lack of sleep was the least of her reasons for contemplating suicide on occasion.

As quietly as she was able, and getting quite adept at it, she slipped from beneath the blanket, careful not to tug or pull to prevent the material rubbing against his skin and startling him awake. With a silent inhalation of relief that he was still snoring, she tip-toed across the tiled floor, cracking with age, and slipped from the room. She peered into the bedroom where her four daughters slept and smiled sadly. Eight years of hell she'd put them through. Staying married to that man made her hate herself but fear choked the life from her nearly every day—fear that he'd carry out his threat to kill her if she tried to leave being at the forefront.

She pulled their door closed, then tip-toed into the computer room, quietly shutting that door behind her. She'd need to do this as quick as possible because if Shane's sleep apnea jarred him awake and he found her missing, he'd come looking for her, and nothing she said would stop his temper flaring. When that happened, it didn't bode well for her, as it generally meant that he'd either try to choke the life out of her or suffocate her with a pillow, just to teach her a lesson.

With exaggeratedly wary movements, she pushed the power button on the Dell desktop and winced when it whirred to life. The noise wasn't overly loud, but in her mind, it rivaled the cheers at a baseball game on opening day. She closed her eyes tight, willing the computer to finish cycling on, then breathed a silent sigh of relief when it quieted, and breathed another when she peered over her shoulder and saw the door to the computer room still closed.

She pressed the button of the monitor and waited impatiently as it too finished its power up. It was nearly instantaneous, but for her it was interminable. The light filled the room and her anxiety elevated. Over the last eight years, she'd attributed superhuman abilities to Shane that didn't truly exist, such as the ability to see the light from her monitor at four in the morning, even though he was fast asleep on the other side of the house. It made her hands shake as her fingers tapped across the keyboard. Normally, she could type 120wpm—a skill she attributed to learning from her mom. One of only a handful of qualities she gave her mom credit for. She rubbed at her temple as her head started throbbing lightly. She was convinced that just thinking about her mom made her head pound. She pushed thoughts of her mom aside. Chanting to herself softly soothing words of comfort, the throbbing subsided slowly, leaving behind a dull ache, which Bethany had long ago learned to live with as that dull ache rarely went away altogether.

She launched the incognito window, and immediately typed "where to purchase thallium" into the search engine. Researching was something that Bethany enjoyed tremendously. Learning something new every day was an adage her father had taught her. It had served her well over the years also, from locating the best car to how to grow tomatoes. It was also an invaluable tool in her arsenal as an author. She thought of the meme she'd seen floating around the internet in which the police were scouring an author's search history to which the author replied, "I swear I'm an author, not a serial killer". That would be her. Only she hadn't spent the better part of a month researching for a novel, rather it was for real life when she typed variations of 'ways to kill someone without leaving a trace.'

Still, if the police ever did suspect her of killing her husband, she initially decided she'd have a plausible reason to present for her search history and then chuckled as another thought popped into her head—she never had a search history.

Life had taught her caution in abundance, which is why she always did her searches in incognito mode and deleted her search history immediately after each session. Nothing ever voluntarily backed up to the cloud. To take it a step further, she scrubbed her computer at the beginning of each month. It was a pain in the rear, covering her tracks so thoroughly, but doing so gave her the confidence needed to research anything, knowing that no one would ever be able to use that research against her. This was especially true for her mom and current husband, both of whom had snooped about on her system a time or two.

When she definitively decided she could murder her husband, her first instinct was to purchase a firearm and shoot him or grab a butcher knife and ram it into his heart. It certainly would've put an end to hers, and her daughters', misery with expediency. It was a thought she began to feed, even convincing herself she'd be able to plead self-defense.

As time progressed and the idea rooted, and began to sprout, taking hold in her mind, she started to worry that a plea of self-defense would be rejected because she had never officially reported Shane's abuse to the police nor even confided to a neighbor. Partly because she wouldn't have a solid explanation as to why she simply didn't leave, and the other was because she knew she'd be told to get a restraining order. That latter resolution wouldn't prevent Shane getting his own firearm and blowing her brains all over their bedroom wall.

So, acting impulsively would invariably see her rotting away the remainder of her life in a prison cell. Thus, the seed that had sprouted, hoping for an expeditious end, quickly withered. That idea may have died away, but her determination to be rid of her husband didn't waver and so she decided to begin researching ways to get away with murder. The answer had been poison.

Yes, it was a bit formulaic. After all, her research also revealed that poison was the preferred method that women elected to use when disposing of their enemies. Still, if she researched it meticulously, wisely, she could find a poison that would be untraceable—or at the very least, wouldn't trace back to her.

Arsenic came to mind, but she discarded that immediately because she was convinced it was one of the first elements for which medical examiners would test for, if police suspected the death was suspicious, and the wife happened to be the prime suspect—which was the case a majority of the time. So that was abandoned as quickly as she thought of it. She'd be suspect one if the medical examiner found arsenic.

Then she stumbled onto a few tidbits of information that caught, and held, her attention. The first was that medical examiners did not test for every poison known to man because it simply wasn't feasible or economical, so unless the death was suspicious, it would likely be ruled as accidental or natural causes. Suspicious, and the tests would likely be limited to the standard and affordable.

Second, there were lethal options available from retailers on the internet that would not likely be tested for in an autopsy. Some were ready to sell to buyers around the world with a few clicks on the keyboard and a valid credit card. More hard-to-obtain products could be found by sellers on the dark web, and this is where Bethany spent the last two weeks trolling for thallium.

Every night, while Shane was at work and the girls were abed, she'd look for sellers, but many were continually out of stock. Made her wonder just how many uses there were for a deadly metal like thallium, or just how many people were buying it for the same reason for which she was.

Her search this night was an act of desperation. She'd never consider sneaking out of bed on a weekend when Shane lay next to her, snoring his head off. But his behavior was becoming more erratic, more dangerous, and she was becoming more desperate to free herself and her girls. It was a risk she felt she had to take.

As she waited for her search query to pop up results, she thought back on the research that led her to thallium and its unique killing power. A radioactive, tasteless, odorless metal of which less than one gram in salt form could kill a person as quickly as firing that firearm that she decided against buying. Better still, it was such a unique killing instrument that it would be unlikely to show up in a standard autopsy.

When she'd first set about searching for sellers, she nearly threw in the towel as it wasn't a substance sold, legally, to consumers. What she didn't expect was to find it available to consumers, illegally. When she began to scour the dark web, she sat back in her chair stunned at having located sellers of the highly illicit substance. She shook her head and sighed loudly, then grinned a grin that would have disturbed her daughters had they seen their mother's face at that moment.

A chime brought her back to the present. The results of her search returned as "limited stock" from one seller. She breathed in deeply and released it slowly in relief, then glanced over her shoulder and glared in self-satisfaction toward her bedroom imagining the pain Shane would suffer if she purchased this and laced his coffee before he headed to work. Would the police suspect a heart attack? Stroke? Since he was a heavy drinker and had the gut to prove it, there was a chance.

She pulled up the seller's information and retrieved the gift card from her desk drawer, given to her a few years back by her employer, an employer that was no more after Shane had called one day, in a drunken rage, and cursed out her boss for no reason. She'd known the reason. Shane had made it clear that he wanted her to stay home with the kids because he couldn't afford childcare. Forget that the childcare was coming out of her salary. When she told him that, he'd found a different excuse—that he didn't want someone else to raise his kids. That didn't work either because, first and foremost, they weren't his kids, nor had he ever treated them as his own. No matter his attempts, Bethany refused to quit because it was a sort of refuge away from him.

He'd put an end to it that day three years ago, calling and cursing out her boss in a nonsensical ramble. It had been humiliating for her, walking into the office the next day to clean out her desk. Her boss had kindly offered to overlook the call and allow her to keep working, but her mortification was too great, so she said goodbye to everyone, less than ten minutes after arriving, and drove the thirty minutes home, fighting back tears of anger.

She'd been home since, tending to her home and children, and writing—both novels and in a journal. Both were cathartic, but Shane nearly ruined that for her also.

She'd awakened earlier than usual one morning. A few minutes before Shane was scheduled home from work. She wasted precious minutes gauging whether she could make it to the bathroom and back before he strolled in. The fear of running into Shane first thing upon waking acting as a paralytic to her limbs. She glanced at the clock once more, decided she had time, threw back the blanket, and dashed across the hall to the bathroom. Halfway back to the bedroom, a light from the computer room caught her eye and she stopped. A little voice warned her not to look, to go back to her bed and wait there as she always did—wait for Shane to crawl into bed and start snoring before going about her day. She didn't listen but wished she had.

Shane was sitting at her computer—reading. The blood drained from her face and she nearly fainted. Her hand shot out instinctively as she fell sideways into the door jamb. The smack against the wood frame was just loud enough to cause Shane to turn in the chair. The look in his eyes caused her feeling of trepidation to intensify. The only thing that kept her from coming out of her skin with worry over what he was reading was her mind reminding her that she'd password protected her journal, so he wasn't reading that, which meant he was just reading one of her novels. That gave her the courage to push away from the wall and walk into the computer room. Still, she couldn't explain the look he was still spearing at her, which was doing its dead-level best to shake her already shaky confidence.

"Why are you reading my stuff? And why are you home from work so early?"

"Not happy to see me?"

"If I meant that, I'd have said that."

"Then where's my kiss?"

"I just crawled out of bed and haven't brushed my teeth yet, Shane. My breath stinks. So, are you going to answer my questions?"

"What? You don't have something on here that I can't look at, do you?"

Realization dawned. The look was no more than a 'gotcha', as if he knew that there was something to find. But if he had, he wouldn't just be asking for a kiss, he'd be threatening to kill her. Of course, she was just so used to seeing threatening looks from him that she could've imagined it altogether. Looking at him now, the only thing glinting from his dark-brown orbs was mischief. He knew he'd been caught but couldn't care less. She did care though. Her writing was her hiding place, a place to escape him, and if he was invading that private space, she'd have nowhere for her mind to run. Not to mention that she needed that outlet to remove the dark thoughts from her psyche.

His snooping on the computer also alerted her to the fact that he'd likely done it before. From that day on, she password protected everything she worked on, downloaded the things she couldn't password protect, scrubbed her search history at shutdown, and scrubbed her hard drive monthly. It was a habit she'd fallen out of when she left home, a habit she started because her mom did the same thing as she'd caught Shane doing—snooping.

By way of explanation that morning though, Shane said that a little bird—later identified as her mom—had whispered in his ear that Bethany was having an affair, and he was just looking for proof.

She wasn't having an affair, of course. Denied it emphatically. Not just because she was innocent of the accusation, but she knew the bodily harm Shane was capable of inflicting on her—and her daughters. The thought had never entered her mind either, as she was far too busy taking care of her children, too drained from trying to live as normally as possible for her children's sake, to even think of starting an affair which she'd then have to hide from Shane.

A strong shudder of remembered fear jolted her back to the present and she realized she'd sat staring at the computer for some time and hadn't yet completed the purchase for the thallium. Panic set in and she prayed that her transaction hadn't timed out.

She lifted the gift card still gripped in her hand, then started punching in the numbers to complete her purchase. She wondered what her former boss would think if he knew what she planned to use the gift card for. It was certainly not what the giver intended when presenting the token of appreciation for all her hard work at her place of employment, but she couldn't think of a better use for it. With a deep inhalation, she hit submit before she could change her mind. She was beginning to feel, with a strange level of certainty, that she'd be able to go through with murder.

Tomorrow though, she planned to make a call to the police, on the recommendation of her oldest daughter. "Just to get it on record, Mom. Just in case he does something stupid."

It had been the growing fear in her daughters' eyes that had finally shaken her from her apathy, or it may have been the breath being choked from her own body when she'd stepped in front of Shane to prevent him assaulting her oldest for having the gumption to stand up to him. Whatever the impetus, she'd finally determined to take that stand, and come hell or high water, she'd free herself and her girls from the grip of that persistently inebriated sod.

With a heavy sigh, she erased her search history as she always did before closing everything down. It was four-fifty in the morning. She'd sat longer than she'd realized but was in no hurry to return to her bed, so she remained a moment longer, staring out at the darkness of the backyard through the partially boarded broken windowpane and sighed again, wistfully this time. She'd purchased this home a couple of years prior to meeting Shane. It was most assuredly a fixer-upper, with its broken windowpanes throughout, it's partially missing floor tiles in all the rooms, the run-down exterior and interior. She closed her eyes at the amount of work still needed to make the place truly habitable but knew she would one day restore it to its former glory.

The first few years, she'd used her federal refund checks to fix something, determined that their home become a place to be proud of. The backyard, though small, made it worth it, for it provided her children with room to run and play, and they made use of it every day. It was one of the things that still brought a smile to her face. Her children were so resilient. Then after she married Shane, he put a stop to the annual improvements, preferring to use the refund on other things. Her half wasn't sufficient for what needed to be done, so she tucked it away in a cash box hidden where Shane would not find it, next to her folder of stories.

Once he was dead and buried, she'd start fixing up the place again.

She opened her eyes and glanced at the clock. Five fifteen a.m. She needed to get back to bed. She rubbed her temples to dispel the onset of yet another migraine, praying that the pain would fade rapidly. They were getting worse. She attributed them to stress over being around Shane too long on the weekends. At least tomorrow the weekend would be over, and Shane would be back at work. She and the girls loathed the weekends because finding ways to avoid Shane for two full days was difficult at best. Bethany stopped and cracked the door to her girl's room one more time, smiling sadly as their breathing reached her ears. "I'll get us free, I promise, and this is one promise I'll make certain to keep. On my life." She pulled the door closed. Tiptoeing across the cool tile floor, she slipped back beneath the blanket, and within minutes was asleep.

Chapter two

Three years later

You're probably asking yourself why you're still sitting and reading the rantings of what you must perceive to be a deranged mind. After all, my husband's death—and that of my mom—should have put an end to it. I should have found peace; a peace I so desperately need. But the ache in my heart and the pain in my head refused to abate, so I decided that I must not be done, and so to rid the world of abusers became a sort of calling, a mission.

I initially started writing about my kills in a journal to purge the filth from my soul, but quite frankly, I have no more words to write because the words used to cleanse became repetitive, because my reason for killing is now superfluous. Thus, the words on the page are a hollow repetition.

I then determined to write my memoirs, as a form of catharsis, to release the burden of my life onto the pages of a book, but after writing a few chapters, something happened, and I found myself questioning my intent. What purpose would the words in a book do for anyone? My pursuit of justice is providing a benefit to society more than any book could do. You see, there are too many women that suffer daily at the hands of the ones they love, from those who profess love in return and no one, but me, appears willing to do anything about it. Therefore, I decided that instead of continuing to free my soul of the malcontent of my actions, I would instead feed that fury and focus it on those who would seek to harm the defenseless, to fight for those who can't fight for

22

themselves, so that is what I've done. A sort of Cat Woman, but without the costume. Why am I sharing any of this with you? Because I wanted you to know that I'm still out here, and I'm not done yet. But what I am done with is trying to go about things surreptitiously. You may not have been aware of my killings before now, but you sure as hell will know who I am going forward, for I intend to ensure that my name becomes etched on your brain; a pain you can't get rid of.

~ Seeker of Justice

Detective Hardwick laid the letter on his desk, his face ashen, his head pounding. He licked his lips, then gnawed on his lower lip as what he just read sank deeper into his soul, killing off what little sympathy he may have felt for the unknown author. He closed his eyes and sucked in a deep breath—he had another serial killer in his district. He was still chaffing over the last serial killer to haunt Atlanta—Christian Price. It was a case that nearly had him tendering his resignation. It gnawed on him like a dog on a bone that justice for those victims had not been meted by his hand. He looked over at his fellow detectives, all working busily trying to close files sitting on their desks. Each had struggled with the Christian Price case, but none had threatened to hand in their badge, as he had. It made him feel ashamed and angry. He'd talked things over with his captain and they'd vowed to change the way in which investigations of that magnitude were handled. Here was their opportunity to see if any of them learned

23

anything at all from their dealings with Price. He'd know soon enough.

He walked over to the copier and copied the pages and the envelope in which they arrived, then placed the pages into an evidence bag. He denoted the date and time, where it was headed and the purpose, signed off on it, and then called over a uniform, "Sign here and then take it to forensics. See if they can pull anything off the pages or the envelope."

The uniform nodded and then Hardwick returned to his desk to make a few notes in the margins. Fifteen minutes later, he returned to the copier to run a few more copies. As the machine hummed, he turned to face his fellow detectives. He wasn't looking forward to this new investigation, was happy with the slew of quickly solved individual homicides that floated in and out of their zone weekly. A sort of rhythm had returned since closing the Christian Price file and he liked it. Far less stress than when dealing with a serial killing psychopath. He sighed heavily as the copier ceased humming.

"Harding, Cortez, Wilson, meet me in the captain's office." He watched, briefly, as each man quickly shuffled their paperwork, closing their current files. Hardwick retrieved the pages from the copier, then headed over to Captain Gary Parsons office. Parsons was the only officer in their unit to have served more time on the force than Hardwick, but only by five years. Stephen Hardwick was a 33-year veteran of the Atlanta Police Department and had quite a few strands of grey hair to prove that his job was not an easy one. The Christian Price case had added more grey hair to his curly mop than any other case in his history.

He knocked on his captain's door and as soon as he heard 'come in' he swung the door open with more force than intended. He took a few breaths and closed his eyes to calm his anger. Parsons knew instantly by not only the look on Hardwick's face, but the tension exuding from his body, that it wasn't good.

"Okay, what've you got?" He asked simply, waving the detectives into his office.

Hardwick started passing out the marked-up copies of the incomplete manuscript and the accompanying letter, "I don't know precisely yet, so your thoughts after you read through this would be appreciated. Do we take her seriously? Or is this 'manuscript' of her life simply a bid for attention to gain notoriety." He compressed his lips and inhaled deeply, then settled on a chair to await their thoughts.

He shook his head slightly as their muttering floated to his ears. *Dear sweet God Almighty, what kind of mom…, is this for real…*were thoughts he too had when he was reading through it so he wondered whether they would also lose sympathy when they reached the final sentences. He wasn't surprised when the words of dismay and disbelief turned to ones of despaired outrage. He nodded, acknowledging their feelings of nausea at having yet another sociopath in the zone.

"It's incomplete?" the captain asked as he flipped the last page.

"Appears to be. It came with a letter which I attached on top. As you can see, it states why she started writing this manuscript, and—"

"She's not done yet," Harding snapped softly.

Each sat in reflective contemplation for a short while, rescanning the pages on their laps until the captain finally regained his voice and spoke up, "I'm assuming these markups are your thoughts on this?" he asked quietly, his normally booming tone tired and subdued.

Hardwick sighed, "Yeah. There aren't many, but I consider them definite points of interest." He looked over at his fellow detectives and asked with a heavy sigh, "We take this seriously?"

"I don't know, man," Harding interjected, shaking his head incessantly, frustration punctuating each word. "I mean, she's talking about killing her mom and her husband in a relatively short span, plus two others—"

"A few years isn't really all that short," Wilson added.

"That, too, is if her dates aren't adjusted to throw us off—how could she possibly kill four people in three years, that she's confessed to, without a hint of it coming to our attention."

"The cases may have come across our desk," Hardwick added. "But ended as cold cases."

"Could be fake," Wilson interjected. "All this could just be her way of getting attention. That five minutes of fame so many people are eager to attain."

"I don't think so," Cortez interjected. "These words are sad and angry, *jefe*, so I think she really intended this to be her memoirs. And if what she wrote about her childhood up to the killings is true…well, she may have started writing about her life growing up and the abuse she suffered at the hands of her mom, and then her husband, which drove her to murder but she ain't over it. Not by long shot."

"Okay, so even if she did kill her mom and husband…and reading what those two put her through, I can't say as I blame her…she doesn't reveal what made her go off on two more people after that—

"If she did," Captain Parsons interrupted. "I'm with Wilson on this one. For this woman to have killed four people without her coming onto our radar as a

27

potential suspect would take a fete of ingenuity that I've not seen in my thirty-eight years on the force.

"Except with Christian Price," Cortez muttered.

"You had to go there?" Wilson snapped.

"Price is behind us, so let's keep him there," the captain replied tightly. "Let's bring our focus back to now, if you please."

"She is less forthcoming on the particulars for those last two murders," Hardwick continued, deliberately ignoring the mention of Price. "Of course, that could be because she doesn't want those details coming back to bite her in the ass. She glossed over those kills to the point that we can't go through the files of unsolved cases to locate them because she provided little-to-no details—"

"True, but she could also have concocted the details related to her mom and her husband," the captain stated. "Also, to throw us off the scent of her trail."

"You think she might be a delusional psychopath?" Hardwick asked.

"Anything is possible," the captain shrugged. "But we can't write her off just yet. There may be a way of confirming at least two of her kills."

"We check the cold case files going back three-five years for incidents related to accidental deaths by

28

chemical fumes, which is how she claimed to have killed her mom—" Hardwick started, and Wilson continued.

"And if we get a hit, we can crosscheck for married children. See if any had a husband die soon after in which the death was ruled as natural causes."

"Think it might be a waste of time to chase down purchases of thallium salt?" Cortez asked, jotting notes and thoughts in the margins of his copy of the letter. "If that's what she really used and didn't just make something up."

"Which is likely—" Wilson started, but the captain interjected.

"I don't think it'll bear fruit, quite frankly. Even if we're to suppose she's giving us facts, and if we just happened to be fortunate enough to find sellers, they aren't doing it legally, which means they aren't going to maintain meticulous records. Most are likely overseas. Plus, that would've been at least three years ago according to her purported memoir. Do you really think you'll find anything? No, the last thing we need is to head down a dead-end street, so let's focus on what can be discovered." Captain Parsons stated, then turned back to his lead detective. "Now, what's this giant circle you have on this map of Atlanta for, Hardwick?"

"She stated that she took her daughters to Café Bourbon the night she poisoned her husband. An impromptu dinner to pass the time until she heard from the police department—"

"Or her husband returned home," Wilson added. "Christ, the fear she must have been living with—"

"—doesn't justify vigilantism," the captain concluded. "Continue Hardwick."

"There's only one location, on Windsor Street. The circle would encompass all possible homes of our killer within that radius, as the crow flies."

"Damn! It'll be a piece of cake locating her for certain. Slam the gavel, case closed," Harding snapped, snarky.

"Easy partner," Cortez soothed, but Harding didn't stop.

"We all know that this map is useless. Hell, she could've driven thirty miles from any direction to reach that place—"

"She said they walked, Harding, remember?" Cortez interjected, but Harding continued as if his partner hadn't interrupted his tirade.

"Being as there's only one of them, she could've driven further, if it was a favorite place of her and her kids. Take into account traffic, traffic lights, construction—which is always going on somewhere— and she could've driven ten miles in five minutes or fifty miles in an hour and a half. Then take into account that this was an account she wrote about from three years ago. Hell, she may have up and moved to Augusta—"

"Jesus, Harding, did you read the manuscript? He circled it because she said that her and her daughters *walked* there," Wilson interrupted, more assertively, "so chill out, will ya?"

"Damn it all to hell and back, Hardwick, why did this have to be delivered to you!"

"I wish I knew, Harding. God knows I wish I knew. The envelope was delivered to the 'detective in charge of the Christian Price case', which means that this person watched that case with intensity. Is maybe even trying to emulate him."

"That may also be why she's sent this to us now."

"I don't understand what you're getting at, Cortez," the captain stated, his brow knitted.

"Just that, if she mentioned that case specifically, even though it's a year past…well…maybe she wants to be the next Price. Maybe she thinks that she deserves the notoriety since she's been, purportedly, killing longer than Price did."

Harding stood abruptly, "I need five, captain." The captain nodded and Harding left the office.

"Want me to go have a chat with him?" Cortez asked.

The captain shook his head, "Nah, he'll be back. He just needs a minute to process this. I think we all do. The last thing we needed, so soon after dealing with Christian Price, is another lunatic."

"If we don't turn up any unsolved cases matching the information in this document, can we assume that this was just an attention-seeking grab and close the book on it?" Wilson asked, and his fellow detectives looked at the captain expectantly.

The captain nodded solemnly, "Yeah, we'll do our due diligence and then put it on the back burner. If a murder gets handed to us, we'll work it as an individual case unless there's something that tells us it's linked to this."

"Let's hope that none get linked," Cortez murmured.

Hardwick drew in a deep breath, his nostrils flaring, "Okay then, I say we scour the case files over a five-year period."

"And what do you propose we do about our current case load?" Harding snapped from just outside the door.

"I get you wanting to tackle this, Hardwick, but any objections to letting some rookies go through the files? Set aside anything of interest we may want to look over later? At least until we're more certain that this is indeed a serial killer and not just some attention-seeking stunt?" The captain asked, not wanting to dismiss his lead detective's concerns over having another potential serial killer. He saw Hardwick stiffen at the mention of turning it over to some rookies since it was a couple of rookies that handed one of Price's victims their death sentence because of a careless oversight. Definitely didn't want that to happen again. He also understood Hardwick wanting to take the driver's seat and get them across the finish line, but at the same time, he couldn't put their current case load aside to chase leads on some cold cases, even if it would potentially mean closing the books on multiple murders. "I'll even supervise," he added when Hardwick remained silent.

After another minute, Hardwick nodded. The other detectives filed out leaving Hardwick and the captain alone.

Hardwick leaned forward heavily on his legs. He lowered his head, shaking it slowly and sighing repeatedly. After a few minutes, he sat back against the chair, "We can't overlook—"

"We won't. I'll make certain of it," Captain Parsons interjected quickly. "I wish I could assuage all your doubts, Hardwick, and I get that mistakes were made during the Price case that cost a woman her life, but we can't move forward assuming that mistakes are going to happen again."

33

"Do you think she meant it when she said she wasn't finished? How many cases have come across our desks over these last three years that were never solved, or were ruled as accidental or natural deaths, that she potentially committed?"

"She only copped to four, Hardwick."

"I know, but her memoir was incomplete—"

"Shit! That's right. She admitted that she stopped writing and then mailed us that incomplete manuscript along with a letter—"

"Which specifically stated that she wasn't done yet. Well, if she isn't done yet *now*, what makes us assume that she wasn't done six months ago, or even last month. If she managed to commit four murders, without us pinning anything on her, in the period covered in that manuscript, what is there to say she didn't kill more people before sending it to me. What's to say that she hadn't killed before her professed murder of her mom and husband; what's to say she hasn't killed since the final two written about in her manuscript."

"Son of a bitch!" Parsons muttered. "You didn't bring this up with the other detectives, why?"

"Because my fears about what she may have done are irrelevant. They aren't facts handed to us to investigate. If we tried to focus on what ifs—"

"We'd get bogged down in a mound of shit so deep we'd not ever find our way out. Maybe fortune will favor us foolish mortals for once and we'll hit pay dirt with those suspicious deaths that remain unsolved. Might even be able to find this woman before the end of the week and sew this up prettier than an embroidered pillow."

At week's end, the only thing to turn up was a dead body with a letter from the manuscript writer, and detectives of the APD's Zone 5 no longer doubted that the author of that work was a fake—nor was she done yet.

Chapter three

Three years earlier

Bethany dried her eyes. Her daughters were due home from school in forty-five minutes and the last thing she wanted was them to see that she'd been crying. That was something she reserved until they were asleep, and Shane was passed out in bed from an overconsumption of vodka—his choice of drink—or at work. He'd be waking in about an hour to get ready for his nightshift at the Federal Express same day customer service center and she wanted to ensure that he didn't see remnants of tears either.

This indulgence in a mid-day sob had to do with the phone call she'd made to the nonemergency number, as she'd been instructed to do by the state patrol office she'd called first. The operator at the local police department had taken her number and told her that she'd have an officer call her back. She'd sat on the front porch for half an hour, wringing her hands, fearful that Shane would wake before she'd had the opportunity to speak secretly to whomever called. It hadn't gone as planned, leaving her feeling angry, saddened, and more vulnerable than she had in quite some time.

She'd explained her situation only to have the officer, in a rather bored and dismissive tone, state that if her husband 'acted aggressively' against her again, to call 911. Until that time, there wasn't anything he could do. Despite her telling him that she simply wanted to get it on the record as instructed by a state trooper, he'd dismissed her with a 'just leave him and file a restraining order' comment.

The shock when he disconnected the call left her staring at the phone for the better part of ten minutes, and then his words sunk in, and the tears started. She wrapped her arms around her midsection and leaned over, feeling nauseated as the tears fell in rivers down her cheeks. But she never uttered a sound. She'd learned that tears could be weaponized against her, giving strength to her abuser. She vowed that was a power Shane would never have over her.

After a few minutes more, she drew in a deep unsteady breath, leaned back, removed her glasses— now drenched and fogged over from the rain of tears— and swiped her eyes dry. She pulled at the hem of her shirt and worked to clean off her lenses, then slid her glasses back on.

She sat staring, hollow feeling, at the weeping willow she'd planted the first week after purchasing the house. Her yard was one of the few things, aside from her children, that made her feel contented and harmonious. Not at this moment, but most days.

The squeal from the air brakes of the school bus jarred her and she blinked rapidly unaware that time had passed. Hearing her daughters' laughter, she quickly stood and ran across the yard to greet them. She was always happy to see them, for in truth it was their faces, shining with the delight from their day, that erased the pain and misery from her heart.

They saw her and ran toward her, yelling "Mom!" and her heart nearly exploded with the love pulsating through it. With a collision that had all of them toppling to the lawn, she forgot about the trauma of the day and her abusive husband and reveled in the laughter and joy of her daughters as she attempted to wrap them all in a single bear hug.

"Okay, okay, y'all win. Let's get up before we get grass stains on our clothes. You do know that your momma is getting way too old for the four of you to keep tackling her like y'all did when you were littler. There'll come a day, in the very near future, that y'all are going to have to make do with good old-fashioned hugs."

Jessica, age fifteen; Katie, fourteen; twins, Julia and Tanya, age twelve, all stood, giggling while brushing the earth from their school uniforms.

The giggles stopped when Bethany opened her mouth again, "Okay, bookbags—"

"On the porch and go to the backyard. We got it, Mom," Jessica finished with a sigh that bespoke of the frustration of their daily routine. It was a practice put in place solely to protect her offspring—conceived with her former husband, Jimmy, who'd been killed in an automobile accident when the twins were but one years old.

Three years after Jimmy's death, Bethany met Shane on a Christian dating site and he'd wooed her with a charm and wit that was irresistible, and their first year of marriage had been pleasant enough. She, and her girls, had done all they could to make him a part of their family, but the red flags started going up when Tanya—who'd just turned five—called him 'dad' for the first time. He'd told her his name was Shane and he wasn't 'dad' to any of them. It had confused Tanya greatly.

Bethany hadn't known at that time that she'd married an abusive alcoholic, and since his drink of choice—she discovered years later—was vodka, there wasn't any tale tell signs to give him away.

But his erratic behavior grew more worrisome as the years passed. He had become not only more physically violent, but verbally abusive also. There were times he'd shout 'bitch' 'whore' or 'cunt' at her and the girls when they were doing no more than jumping on the trampoline.

Another tactic she employed to protect them, in addition to sending them out back after school, was to wait until he tumbled into bed after his overnight shift before arising to get the girls ready for school. It never took long for him to start snoring, but because it was after seven a.m., Bethany had little time to get the girls up and ready. Being as quiet as possible, they'd tiptoe around as fast as they could—dressing, combing their hair, and brushing their teeth.

Some mornings, he stayed awake too long, so the girls would have to brush their teeth in the car, because Bethany would wake them just long enough to dress and shuffle them out the door to drive them to school. On those mornings, however, to lighten the rude awakening, she'd run them by McDonalds for a big breakfast before taking them in, inevitably late.

The routine made the weekdays more tolerable because with the late rise and then playing outside directly after school, the girls didn't have to face Shane hardly at all, and Bethany was only subjected to his snide assaults for an hour or less before he stormed from the house and headed off to work. It was the weekends that were the hardest on them all.

"He hasn't left yet?" Katie asked softly as they all moved sluggishly toward the house.

"Sweetie, you know that he doesn't leave until about an hour after you get home."

"Yeah, but I can dream, can't I?"

"Definitely don't stop dreaming. Now scoot. I'll bring y'all a snack."

The twins bounced after their older sisters, mimicking them in most everything, except in the shroud of sadness that fell over the two older girls at having to be home and exiled to the backyard for the next hour. A shroud that would quickly lift once allowed back inside. It was the same for Bethany as she trudged to the front door, scooping up the backpacks dumped onto the front steps.

She sighed heavily and mentally put on her shield before stepping inside, knowing that she would need it as soon as Shane got up. She pulled open the screen door and stopped dead in her tracks, her mouth gaping, as she watched Shane—who'd awakened early—pick up her beloved eleven-year-old Dalmatian Pointer mix, Zeus, and toss him unceremoniously onto the floor. He turned and saw her rooted there and snapped, "Keep that fucking dog off my couch. Isn't it time you got rid of that mutt?"

No, but it's time to get rid of you, Bethany thought, wishing she had the courage to speak the words aloud. "I've had Zeus with me far longer than you've been in my life," she said with far more bravado than she felt. *And he'll be with me long after you're gone,* she concluded tacitly, dropping the bookbags on the floor beside the front door.

Shane grinned wickedly, "Yeah, maybe, but I'm not the one going anywhere anytime soon." The fact that he stated something contrary to her thoughts made her shudder, wondering whether he could read her thoughts, as he often threatened that he could do. It also made her fear for her pet's life, as his words sounded so much like the veiled threats that he often aimed at her.

"Zeus isn't going anywhere, that's for certain." It made her ill whenever something helpless got bullied by someone who should know better. Keeping the girls out of Shane's reach was easier than an animal who simply didn't comprehend the danger.

Bethany's nerves were rattling as she turned to follow Zeus who'd ambled off toward the kitchen. She needed to check on her aging pet, but she also wanted to put distance between her and a man she'd come to detest in the short eight years they'd been married. Avoidance was becoming par for the course because staying in his company for any length of time was wearing on her. The term 'walking on eggshells' had changed its meaning over the years. It was now akin to tiptoeing on grenades, as Shane's behavior appeared to be degenerating more swiftly with each passing year.

Bethany had just stepped into the kitchen when a large, beefy hand reached around from behind, grabbed her by the throat, and spun her around, slamming her against the doorjamb. The impact was so great that her breath left her in a whoosh. The pressure against her

42

throat made drawing air into her lungs impossible and soon stars began filling her field of vision; a sign that unconsciousness was rapidly approaching. She heard Zeus start barking, but the sound was muted, as were the sounds of the girls calling for her because they'd heard Zeus's distress from the backyard and were headed inside.

The thought of the girls moving into harm's way elevated her panic and in a feeble attempt to break free, if only to protect her babies from Shane, she raised her hands and tried to pry his huge fingers from around her neck. All the while, Shane just stood staring at her, voicing not a word. His dark eyes glinting as he appeared entranced by her struggles to live. After a minute, he leaned down to whisper, "This is the only way you'll be leaving me."

"Let go of our mom," Jessica screamed, slamming the full force of her one-hundred-thirty-pound body into Shane's legs. It had little effect on his bullish two hundred thirty-pound frame, but it did seem to jar him from his trancelike state, and his hand fell away from Bethany's throat. She sank to the floor sucking in deep breaths, coughing as the air worked its way painfully back into her lungs.

She prayed desperately to regain her zapped strength rapidly as she watched, through star-filled vision still blurred from lack of oxygen, as Shane turned on the girls, who'd backed themselves into the corner, the three youngest huddling together and crying.

Jessica, who'd landed on her bottom when she collided with Shane, scooted backwards to join her sisters as if suddenly aware that her courageous act would have dire consequences. Zeus, sensing distress in the girls, leapt in front of them, pushing against them, snarling, and snapping at Shane's approach.

"I'll snap your arthritic hide in two, dog," he growled with a tone that bordered on glee. The girls began to wail louder, and Jessica got up onto her knees to wrap her arms around Zeus. She pulled him backwards, begging him to stop snarling and snapping because she didn't want him to get hurt. The pleading made Shane laugh.

The crying pleas of 'mommy' from the twins were making Bethany's heart hammer loudly against her chest. It also gave her the impetus needed to shake the fog from her brain and she grabbed hold of the doorknob and pulled herself up onto unsteady legs. She stumbled toward where her children cowered, nearly falling onto her knees, standing by sheer will alone. With a loud hoarse roar, she rammed into Shane, sending him stumbling into the stove. She closed the distance to the girls, reached over and grabbed a butcher knife from the dish strainer, then turned around, teetering, still drawing giant breaths into her lungs—to rid her vision of the

44

persistent stars and to calm her runaway nerves. She leaned back against the counter to stabilize herself, but jutted her chin forward in defiance and brandished the knife in front of her like a shield. When he didn't react the way she'd hoped—which was fearfully—she pushed herself away from the counter and took a timorous, unstable step closer, all the while forcing herself to hold the knife steady.

"I could make you eat that knife, you know," Shane sneered derisively.

"Not before I made you bleed," Bethany breathed hoarsely.

Standing tremulously next to Zeus, in front of her daughters, she knew with unfailing certainty, when Shane just grinned, that she'd have to take matters into her own hands if she were going to break free from him. She'd sought justice from their local police and received no help. Now it was up to her, and if it meant stabbing him in the heart if he took a step closer to them, then by God she would.

"You haven't got it in you, bitch."

"Make no mistake, Shane, that if I have to use this I will."

Something in her tone must have startled him because in a move that surprised her, Shane turned swiftly and left the kitchen, but he did so with his daily

45

warning—try to leave and he'd hunt them down and kill them all. She knew he meant it, which is why she knew that a restraining order would be useless. Not that she had anywhere to go or enough money to get there. That left her only one recourse—she had to move forward with her plans to use the thallium. She couldn't chance it any longer.

Twice in less than a month, he'd attempted to strangle her. Last week, he drove his car into the backyard where she'd been working and attempted to run her over. The weekend before that, he'd forced her to perform fellatio before pushing her off his flaccid member in anger after nearly twenty minutes of trying to achieve an erection. He pushed her onto her back then sat on top of her, making it difficult to draw breath. He then reached over and grabbed his pillow, "What good are you if you can't do nothing but lie here like a plank? Better off dead." He brought the pillow down heavily onto her face, chuckling when she started trying to buck him off. She managed to turn her head sideways to keep from suffocating, but likely would have had he not suddenly passed out himself—drunk as a skunk, as the saying goes.

The verbal and physical attacks were becoming more frequent, more violent. As scared as she'd been when he threatened her daughters with brutality if she tried to leave him, the fear of dying and leaving them alone with him left her horrified. If he discarded them, refused the responsibility of caring for them, that would leave them in the care of her mother, or foster care, and that—to Bethany—was a fate just as bad.

Today's incident was the slap across the face that she needed to do something, because if she didn't kill him, he'd surely kill her.

A few minutes later, the front door slammed, and the engine of their Oldsmobile Cutlass Supreme roared to life. A collective sigh of relief filled the air and the tension melted away. Bethany turned to her girls who immediately jumped up and wrapped their arms around her. Even Zeus felt the difference in the atmosphere and began wagging his tail and licking at the girls' faces.

Bethany sank to her knees as the relief spreading through her body weakened her legs even more. She petted Zeus's head, "You did good, boy. No tears, girls. We aren't going to do this for much longer. It's taken a while, but I finally found an out. Just give it a week and we'll be free."

"You promise?" Katie asked softly.

"With every fiber of my being."

The phone rang, causing all five of them to jump. Each let loose a nervous giggle. Bethany got up to answer the phone, but the girls' refusal to let go of her made it difficult. She didn't tell them to let go. She just

47

shimmied across the kitchen floor, hugging them with as much need as they gripped her. If the caller decided to disconnect their call, that was fine by her. Instead, the ringing persisted until she was able to grab the receiver.

"Hello," she breathed heavily.

I need help. Get over here!

"If you need help, mom, call 911. I'm busy."

The girls released her suddenly as if the taint of their grandmother would transfer from the phone to their mom and infect them. Each watched their mom's face warily, watching for additional signs of distress. None had seen their grandmother in six years, and none wanted to. She treated them with just as much vile as did Shane and they wanted nothing to do with her. Knowing how she'd treated their mom her entire life made them revile the woman even more.

I don't need no strangers tramping around my house. Just get in the car and get over here. I just need help getting up.

The line disconnected and Bethany drew in a deep breath through her nostrils.

"You're not going over there, are you, mom?" Katie asked, trepidation lacing her tone.

"You know you always come home in a bad mental place whenever you go over there," Jessica added.

48

"She just needs help getting off the floor. Won't be gone long," Bethany sighed heavily, heading for the front door.

"You can't go," Julia interjected smugly. "Shane took the car, remember?"

To the other three girls, this was a great point, and they praised Julia for coming up with it. This meant that their mom would be safe from the tongue-lashing that she was bound to get from their grandmother if she went over there. To them, she got enough of that from their stepfather.

"Y'all know it's walking distance, and it's still light out. I'll get there and back long before dusk. Okay? Don't worry, I'll carry my shield. Her words won't get through that."

"Nice try, mom," Tanya snorted.

"We should at least go with you," Jessica offered, half-heartedly.

This made Bethany grin wryly, "and get hit with those barbs meant for me? I've only got one shield, you know. It can't provide cover for all of us. I'll be back soon. Y'all put something together for dinner. I should be back within the hour."

Before her daughters could protest further, Bethany headed out the front door. She wasn't really eager to go to her mother's aid, but she didn't want

49

anyone accusing her of elder neglect. If it meant protecting her children, she'd gladly suffer the abuse. Besides, in her mind, she'd suffered abuse from her mom for her entire life, so it was nothing new. Her shield might be imaginary, but the wall she'd built around herself to defend from her mom's assaults was as real as could be.

She'd been the focus of her mom's vicious verbal assaults from the time she was old enough to know what a back-handed compliment was, and to discern derision in words. The physical assaults didn't happen often, but they were frequent enough to leave their mark, since her mom would take a belt to her backside every chance she got, whether it was something she did accidentally or if she was simply mad at the neighbor for playing music too loud—Bethany was the outlet for her rage. A rage which grew when her dad left.

Bethany's mom blamed her daughter for that too, yelling that it was she who caused their divorce— and for once, she'd been right.

Bethany had been sitting at the piano—her hiding place—when her dad approached her, asking her to sign something. Bethany loved her dad dearly and readily did so. Half hour later, her mom was in her face screeching like a banshee, "I hope you're proud of yourself, you little troublemaker, 'cause you just signed our divorce."

The accusation hadn't broken Bethany, but her dad leaving her behind, never to contact her again, had. She became a hollow shell, avoiding her mom as much as was able, until the day she turned eighteen and fled the house, straight into the arms of her future husband, Jimmy. For a few short years, she'd found peace and happiness with her husband, and each of her children. She wrapped herself in the cloak of their love, absorbing it to heal her wounds, which ran deep. She even managed to be around her mom—on the rare occasion—because the love in her heart acted as a shield against the taunts hurled at her at every opportunity. Jimmy also defended her, which shut her mom up and that made her love him all the more.

Then catastrophe struck, when a drunk driver slammed into Jimmy while he was on an evening walk. Her world shattered.

When she'd met Shane three years later, she hoped that he would be the same healing force in her life as had been Jimmy and her children. Instead, he'd turned out to be mom number two and between the two of them, they'd worked to destroy what joy she worked hard to maintain in her life. If attacking her didn't work, they went after her babies. Belittling them with their every breath.

Eight years on, after living in purgatory, which created a pounding in her head and an ache in her heart that refused to abate, realization dawned: she was indeed capable of murder.

Chapter four

Bethany walked up the driveway of her mom's house half an hour later, drawing in deep calming breaths. No matter how hard she attempted to put the past behind her, it always managed to creep into her soul and rattle her but good—especially when she was pulled back into the hell that was her mother's sphere. She rubbed at the throbbing in her temples and picked up her pace. The sooner she got in there, got her mom off the floor, the sooner she could get home to her babies.

"Mom, it's me. Where are you?" she called as she entered the front door, which was never locked. Bethany couldn't count the number of times that she'd wished a thief would walk in that unlocked door and shoot her mom, killing her on the spot. She often told herself that she should feel guilty over such a thought, but since it was just a thought, she refused to allow herself to hold onto any feelings of guilt.

"Get your lazy, sorry ass in here, girl!"

Bethany closed her eyes as the words slammed into her and then remembered that imaginary shield that she teased her daughters about. She took a deep breath, released it slowly, then raised that imaginary shield as she walked toward the loud, exaggerated, dramatic moaning emanating from the bathroom. By the time she traversed the short distance, she was grinning, but no amount of breathing ever seemed to relieve the throbbing in her head.

"What are you grinning like an idiot for? Dimwit. Wipe that smirk off your face and help me off the floor. I've been down here for ages. What took you so long? Take the long way on purpose, I bet? You just like to see me suffering, don't you? Where's Shane? Why didn't you bring him along? You ain't strong enough to lift me off no floor, girl!"

Bethany wished she could say 'shut up' in the manner in which her deceased husband used to do. Jimmy could shut her up easily. Send her skulking out of the room too. The first time Bethany had tried that, all it managed to do was to have her mom start swinging her cane at her head. Her mom might be getting up in age, but she had a good forty pounds on Bethany and used that added weight to her advantage.

This had been one of the only times she'd stepped foot in her childhood home, on her own. She would never have come back at all if Shane hadn't got some perverse joy out of dragging her there every Sunday. He used to make the girls come too, until they got old enough to stay home without supervision. That's when Bethany had put a stop to them coming. Shane had threatened to make things even more difficult for her and her daughters if she refused to go with him though. So, she went and would just sit off in a corner making as small a target as able. Her mom and Shane were cut from the same cloth—black wool spun from the fires of Hell—and they enjoyed each other's company tremendously.

"Shane had only just left for work when you called. Guess you should've fallen a bit sooner if you'd wanted his help," Bethany said, her tone as dead as her love for the woman sitting in a heap next to the toilet.

"Shoulda just called 911 for all the good you'll do me," her mom snorted.

"Then maybe you should. Your phone's right there next to you on the floor. They should be here in about an hour." Bethany turned to leave.

"You leave me here, I swear I'll call CPS on you. Tell them you abuse me just like you do them brats of yours."

Bethany stopped walking and closed her eyes, breathing slowly, counting to ten repeatedly to keep from losing her cool. After years of having CPS visit her home to follow up on an anonymous tip, she had no doubt that her mom would indeed follow through with that threat.

A tear escaped and Bethany's cool shattered.

She turned on her mom, reached down and picked up her cell phone, placing it deliberately on the floor out of her reach. She then walked zombie-like around the house, collecting supplies, ignoring her mom's demands to tell her what she was up to.

"I don't know what you're up to, you selfish little brat, but whatever it is, you'll end up regretting it."

Bethany compressed her lips into a thin line of anger and determination. She placed a bucket near her mom's feet, which her mom kicked over immediately. With a grin, she poured bleach and ammonia into the bucket, dropped a sponge inside, placed it by her feet again, then quickly stepped out and shut the door behind her.

Her mom's screams followed her from the house, but when Bethany closed the front door, the sounds became too muted to hear. That assured her that no neighbors would be coming to her aid.

True to her word, the time it took for Bethany to make the trip to and from her mom's house was less than an hour.

Her countenance lit up, as did her heart, as soon as she walked into her own home and saw the simple dinner her children had prepared for her.

"You okay, mom?" Jessica asked.

"Couldn't be better, now that I'm home. Let's eat."

Chapter five

Bethany stood staring at the packet in her hand.
Her order for thallium had arrived far sooner than
anticipated and she found herself, once again, struggling
with her looming decision. It had only been two days
since Shane had attempted to strangle the life out of her,
two days since she'd vowed to herself—and her
children—that the abuse would end soon. Two days
after proving to herself that she was capable of murder.
Of course, she didn't know if her mother was dead. For
all she knew, someone could've have discovered her
mother, and she was alive and well in some hospital bed.
Of course, that would mean that the cops could come
knocking on the door for her soon and that meant she
needed to take care of Shane in all haste. She couldn't
risk him living, to care for her children if she were
arrested for assaulting her mom—or worse, murdering
her. She hated unknowns, and this one was huge for
her.

Still, the knowledge that she was capable of
killing was new to her and that warred with her brain,
which shouted that she had to act. Those same logic
circuits in her brain were also warring with the
emotional center of her heart. If she was caught and
arrested, she could lose her children forever. True,
Shane wouldn't be able to hurt them any longer, but

they'd be placed somewhere and there was no guarantee that place would make them happy.

Worse still, if Shane did die opportunely, after her vow they'd be rid of him soon, would her children look at her in suspicion, wondering if she'd done something nefarious? Would she be able to look at herself in the mirror every day after and not see a villain far worse than Shane?

The girls were out back jumping on the trampoline. She could hear their laughter drifting in through the back door and she closed her eyes and soaked it in. Their resilience through these years was an inspiration to her that life didn't end because of violence.

"Unless that abusive spouse murders you," she muttered and thought of all the other women—and men—in similar circumstances who were trapped with no one to save them. That was all the impetus she needed. No one was going to be there to save her the next time Shane decided to act with lethal aggression. Her heart burned with savage rage as she ripped open the package and pulled out the tiny vial of thallium salt. She dumped the contents into the bottom of Shane's travel mug and set about making his daily coffee.

As the Keurig spit out the hot brew into the mug, Bethany breathed slowly in and out through her nostrils, stirring the black liquid to aid in the amalgamation of the poison. She tore open four packets of Splenda, then added his preferred hazelnut creamer, praying that either or both would mask any off-putting taste that would cause Shane not to drink it.

Her greatest fear as she continued to stir, check, and stir some more, was the metallic salt crystals would not dissolve. She nearly started crying when they did, leaving only a grey haze floating on the liquid surface. She capped the mug and again closed her eyes in supplication that he'd not notice anything off when he drank it.

She hated that this, if it worked as advertised, would likely result in him crashing her Oldsmobile, her only means of transportation, and prayed that if it did happen when he was driving across town that no other people would be impacted. It was one thing to rid the world of a brutally abusive bastard, it was another for there to be fatalities of innocents.

She rubbed firmly at her temples as another migraine threatened to take hold. The headaches were becoming more frequent and more intense. She hoped and prayed that once she dealt with Shane, they would cease. As soon as he left, she'd pop a couple of Aleve.

"Are you going to stare at it until it's too cold to drink?" The baritone voice standing so near to her startled her so that she knocked the mug off balance, nearly making a mess of her kitchen floor—and her plans. She grabbed the mug, grateful for her lightning-fast reflexes, and felt her temper elevate when she heard Shane chuckling behind her. She wanted nothing more than to take the coffee and throw it in his face. Instead, she did as she always did—tamp down hard on her emotions. Push them so deep that no amount of provocation from Shane would bring them to the surface. She drew in some deep, slow breaths, then turned to hand the mug to him, her expression devoid of emotion.

Shane noticed her blank expression and sneered in derision. He hated that he couldn't get the rise out of her that he wanted, hated knowing that the minute he walked out the door her vapid expression would vanish and be replaced with smiles and laughter with the brats out back. Hated more than anything the feeling that the control he wielded was slipping from his grasp. He'd get it back, he vowed, by whatever means were necessary.

"Don't forget my kiss," he murmured, the threat in his tone daring her not to. Bethany's nostrils flared, but she leaned up and planted a quick kiss on his lips. One of the first things that Shane had told her when they married was that he was never to leave for work without her kissing him goodbye. He'd made it a requirement, and one that she grew to loathe.

She'd defied that command only once by heading out front to check the mail just as he was getting ready to leave. She'd stood at the mailbox as long as she could until she saw him storm from the house and head straight for his little red Honda Civic—which he wrecked a week later. He must have spotted her as he backed out of the driveway because he stopped as soon as he backed onto the main roadway—and so did her heart, as she watched him glare at her from the driver's seat. She raised her chin and started to move back toward the house when he suddenly accelerated, grazing her hip as he shot past her. That day, she'd suffered no more than a massive bruise; that day she'd realized just what he could do to her if she defied him again. So, she complied with his 'kiss' demand, remaining defiant only deep within her soul.

"See you in the morning."

From a loving spouse, this would have been a looked-forward to time but hearing those words every evening from Shane was a threat compounded upon threat. Every word from his mouth was laced with menace meant to terrorize her. So, every evening she'd hold her breath in anticipation of the front door closing and the car starting. Then and only then was she able to release the pent-up tension and begin to relax.

Tonight, however, she wanted to see him leave; hoped to catch a glimpse of him sipping his coffee before he backed out of the driveway. Only then would she have hope that their nightmare of a life would soon be over.

The moment she heard the front door close, she raced to the window and peered from behind the curtain. He climbed into the driver's seat and leaned back but didn't immediately start the car. Instead, he leaned his head against the headrest and closed his eyes. Bethany's brow knitted, worried that his actions somehow meant he wasn't going to leave. Did he do this every time he got into the car? She had no clue what his daily routine was. Her heart began palpitating strongly in her chest.

"Please, pick up…" the entreaty no sooner began than she saw him lift the mug and take a huge gulp. She drew in a sharp breath through her nose and slowly released it then repeated it when he took another long drink from the mug. After one more drink, he sat the mug down, turned the key in the ignition and backed out of the driveway, with his routine squeal of tires on the gravel. A moment later he was away.

Bethany dropped the curtain and sank to her butt, drawing her knees to her chest and lowering her head. She didn't know how to feel. Too many emotions were warring within her at that moment: relief and guilt the top two.

She'd only ever thought about taking the life of another person. From insulting past boyfriends who wanted nothing from her but sex, to the pastor in the pulpit who'd pointed a finger at her when she'd first attended and told her she was welcome there if she didn't get involved with any of the male congregants. She'd come to find out later that he thought she was a divorcee, when in fact she was a widow. The thought of divesting the world of these people often floated through her brain, but kept on moving, rarely stopping to take root—until her mom and Shane, seemingly working in concert, had pushed her over the edge. Of course, her mom had been shoving her toward that very edge since childhood. She'd just never been able to push hard enough to send her over into the murderous abyss. The two of them together, however…

She was working hard to resolve her feelings when another joined the fray: fear. A fear that jarred her so strongly that her heart began to race, and beads of sweat popped out on her brow. The fear that Shane could survive. After all, she hadn't thought to research whether the efficacy of thallium would be diluted if mixed with hot liquids—like his coffee. Just like the fear that woke her at two a.m. night-before-last that her mom could've survived.

Her research gave her a strong indication that the thallium would kill him, but she wouldn't know for certain until the police showed up on her doorstep—or he came strolling through the door tomorrow morning, alive and well.

63

The pain in her head intensified and she closed her eyes against the assault on her nerves. "I can't…if I sit here dwelling on what ifs, I'll lose my mind." Bethany pushed up from the floor. "I've got to get out of here." She strolled through the kitchen and out to the backyard, grabbing a bottle of Aleve along the way. She struggled to work off the child-proof cap and was nearly cursing by the time it popped free. She turned the bottle over and sighed in aggravation when the last three blue tablets fell into her palm, "Gotta get more already. Shane better die, if only to ease these headaches and the strain on my wallet."

"Hey mom, come jump with us!" Julia shouted as she bounced into the air.

"How about instead we walk to Café Bourbon for dinner," Bethany called with a forced cheeriness, stopping on the back step. She stuffed the empty Aleve container into her pocket and prayed the pills she popped would start working soon.

"Really? But it isn't Friday," Tanya called, scrambling off the trampoline, followed quickly by her sisters.

"Yeah, mom, what gives?" Jessica asked as they all ran up to her.

"If y'all don't want to go, we can always stay here and enjoy my Raman and hotdogs," Bethany threatened

64

teasingly, not really wanting to justify the abrupt change to their routine.

"Nope, nope, nope, and nope," Katie replied emphatically. "I want bourbon."

Bethany snorted, "God, child. The things you say."

"Will we still get to go tomorrow too?" Julia inquired, as they filed inside.

"Hmm…I'll have to think about that, but we're definitely going to today, so go get a baby wipe and clean up a bit, then we'll get walking.

There was a unified 'yay' as the girls dashed across the yard to the house, and all tried to file into their single bathroom at the same time to grab a baby wipe. The play bickering and ensuing laughter would normally cause a smile to play across her lips, but her pounding head, instead, made her want to duct tape their mouths closed.

While they were in the bathroom, Bethany picked up the phone and dialed her mom's cellphone. If she'd survived…this was one way she felt she could know. No answer. She disconnected and realized that she never called her mom, so she didn't know if she had a habit of ignoring her phone or not. Should she phone the police? Feign concern? Have them check in on her. Welfare check. It would certainly remove suspicion from her if she was dead. She made a mental note to call tomorrow. Tonight, she needed to get past what she'd done to Shane—well deserved as it may be.

She breathed deeply in and out, closing her eyes against the pain. She settled onto the couch to await the girls. When she opened her eyes, Jessica was standing in front of her, her brow knitted with concern.

"You okay, momma?"

Bethany smiled thinly, "Just a mild headache, sweetie. Probably just need to eat something, so if you girls could hustle…" She hadn't even managed to finish her sentence before the four whirlwinds were out the front door. "Who wants to be the head of the triangle today?" She called to Jessica and Katie as she followed them out of the house. The triangle had been their way of allowing the twins a bit of freedom during walks when they were younger. One of the older girls would walk to the front of the twins and Bethany and the other would walk behind. The twins had been taught that they weren't to leave the triangle this formed, or they'd have to hold someone's hand for the duration. It was a lesson they took to quickly and never once had they strayed from the safety of the triangle.

It was also something that became a habit on their walks and just something they did instinctively now.

It was less than a twenty-minute walk to the eatery, but it was all the time needed for Bethany to unwind after a stress-filled week—or in this case, a stress-filled few days. Walking and focusing on her daughters were surefire ways for her to push her fears to the back of her mind—for now—and it was working on reducing the pain in her skull, along with the Aleve she'd taken.

By the time the five of them had eaten dinner and started back to their small abode, Bethany had all but forgotten that she'd poisoned her husband over an hour and a half before. She was smiling ear-to-ear, and shaking her head in wonder, as she always did when listening to her daughters go on about something or other that made little sense to her. Still, they brought her peace.

That peace was shattered when they turned from Tift Avenue onto Lillian Avenue. They still had a few blocks to walk, but there was no way to mistake from where the flashing red lights illuminated. The girls knew it too.

"Mom? Is that a cop car at our house?" Jessica queried, inexplicably nervous. "What do you think they want?"

"Hopefully to tell us that Shane is dead," Bethany muttered unintelligibly.

"Huh?"

67

"Nothing that we did," she stated emphatically, "so nothing to worry over. Let's get there and find out what's going on." Bethany couldn't explain to her daughters her sudden anticipatory mood any more than she could explain it to herself. Part anxiety and part hope was all she could figure. She simply felt a sudden jolt in her body that had her feet moving at a faster clip, making it difficult for the twins to keep up. As always, Jessica and Katie were there to attend. When they'd been younger, Jessica and Katie would simply scoop Tanya and Julia into their arms, but now they simply snatched one of the twins' hands, pulling at them to ensure they didn't fall behind.

As they crossed the lawn, a member of the Atlanta Police Department strode over to meet them.

"Mrs. Barnstead?"

"That's right. What can I do for you, officer?"

"I'm Officer Carter and this is my partner, Officer Turner. Do you mind if we step inside?"

Bethany's brow knitted, but as she glanced about and noticed her neighbors lining the sidewalk, she nodded. She appreciated her neighbors. They were generally there for each other, but none knew of the abuse she'd suffered at the hands of her husband. That was a private matter she kept closely guarded. And if the officers were there to tell her what she thought they were, she didn't want—or need—anyone trying to console her. How could she explain that she wouldn't need consolation, that she'd feel more like celebrating.

She nodded to the officers, then headed for the house. Her steps faltered slightly when she realized that the police could be there to simply inform her that they'd located her mother's body. Shane could very well still be alive and well. This caused her temper to flare momentarily and her normally gentle instruction to her daughter ended coming out curter that usual, "Jessica, take your sisters out back."

"But momma—" Jessica started to complain. She wanted to know what was going on.

"Now, Jessica. Do as I say. I'll call y'all in when I think it's a good time."

"Let's go, y'all," Jessica huffed, heading for the back gate. Bethany watched them disappear into the backyard, then headed up the steps to the house, drawing deep calming breaths in and out of her nostrils. She was nowhere near being an actress and her brain ran amok over whether she'd be able to pull off the part of a grieving widow—or grieving daughter, whichever the case might be.

Zeus immediately set to barking at the officers as they entered the living room, which gave Bethany a much-needed distraction from her worried mind.

"Just give me a minute to put him out back with the girls," she said. Taking Zeus by the collar, she led him through the kitchen out the back door, "Y'all keep an eye on Zeus, will ya?"

"Yes, momma," Katie called, as she bounced high into the air.

"You just ate not too long ago, so don't go doing something that's going to make you throw up," she called. "Y'all make a mess on that trampoline, you're hosing it off, not me."

She turned back to go talk to the officers but stopped in the kitchen and closed her eyes against the assault of nervousness rampaging through her body. She tried her Zen breathing and even began mentally stomping on her emotions, to push them deep into the gut, as she did time and again when dealing with Shane, but as she lifted a hand to wipe the beads of sweat away from her upper lip, she couldn't help but notice her hand trembling.

"Get a grip, girl. They ain't gonna arrest your ass unless you give them a reason to suspect you done something stupid, which you know you didn't. Righteous, yes. Stupid, no." Her mental chastisement worked, and she felt the tension slowly seeping away. "Just please be here to tell me that Shane is dead." She breathed in a deep, calming breath, then headed to the living room.

"What can I do for you, officers? Has something happened?"

Officer Carter leaned forward slightly, "We're sorry to inform you that your husband died this evening—"

"Did that son-of-a-bitch go and crash my Oldsmobile?" Bethany exclaimed. It was out of character for her to be so crass, but it was the only way she could think of to find out if her only means of transportation was gone. "Wait a minute! Did you say died?" She added, then grinned internally thinking she might just be able to give an Oscar-worthy performance after all.

"He wasn't in an accident—"

"What the hell happened?" *Easy, Bethany, don't go overboard. You don't want them thinking you ain't right somehow,* she mentally reprimanded. "I'm sorry, I don't mean to keep interrupting you. It's just…um…what happened?"

"We don't know for certain. Possibly a heart attack…"

Bethany stopped listening. Their words didn't matter now. All that mattered was that she'd won and since they weren't there to arrest her, she was going to get away with it. She felt a vindicated relief sweep over her. For most of her life she'd suffered abuse at the hands of one person after another, but now that was over. It was just her and her girls now, and she vowed, then and there, never to let anyone hurt any of them again.

She thought of the men and women in her abuse chat room, wishing she could give them her secret so they could free themselves, but knew it wasn't possible. This was a secret she'd have to take to her grave if she wanted to live this day onward for her daughters. Then another thought flitted through her mind, *Why can't I help them as I did myself?* That thought would set her on a collision course with justice.

It was a mere two days later that the same officers returned to notify her that her mother's body had been found by a member of her church congregation. Despite the coincidence—apparent to herself, at least—she hadn't been considered a suspect in either death. All the officers had done was offer their sincere condolences over the loss of two people in her life.

The coroner had ruled Shane's death as natural causes and her mother's as accidental. This had enabled Bethany to collect the life insurance from both. She'd known of Shane's policy, through his employer, but was stunned when she'd found the policy in her mother's effects, a week later, naming her as beneficiary. She'd despised her mom, and had no doubt her mom felt likewise, but the money from both policies ensured she'd be able to care for her daughters securely until they were able to fly the coop and get jobs of their own.

That was, as long as she didn't do anything stupid—like get caught.

Chapter six

Three years later

Atlanta has grown so much in the last decade. It's spreading like octopus tentacles. No, I don't like that analogy. An octopus, after all, is only an animal but Atlanta is more like a cancer, spreading incurably, infecting other smaller towns as it pulls them into its grasp. Like the dictator of a country who has the sickening need to conquer and assimilate. I must admit, it does make it easier to locate and eradicate those blights whose very existences are an abomination to humanity. Just take a drive down any street these days and you'll encounter all sorts of riff raff who need more than just an attitude adjustment.

Take, for instance, this fellow. I'm just driving along, minding my own business, when I see him out front—in his briefs of all things—smacking the shit out of his Pitbull with a belt. I don't know what that poor animal did to deserve such treatment, and I may have been of a mind to mind my own business had the dog been in a position to bite back. Instead, it can't run because it's on a tie-down and it can't bite or even bark a warning because it's muzzled. Doesn't seem much like a fair fight to me. And as I pulled along the curb, watching in abject horror, I was thinking that if he could do that to his dog, he's just as likely to do that to his wife or kids, when lo and behold, a woman, clad in nothing more than a silk teddy comes scampering outside to try to stop the abusive treatment.

Uncaring of her own safety, bless her, she leapt between the man and the whimpering bull terrier and met the wrath of the

74

man who didn't even pause in his onslaught, inflicting her with the same violence. Only she wasn't muzzled, so her yelps brought forth the neighbors. Even I, who knew not this woman at all, stepped from my car ready to fight her battle alongside her...but all I could do was step away and allow those who knew her best to rush to her and her beloved pet's aid as the man stormed back inside.

Well, I'm certain as can be that he felt equally helpless before I was done with him. I wasn't in a position to help her then, but that didn't stop me helping her later. He certainly won't be beating on any more helpless creatures—or his wife—ever again, that's for damned sure.

Oh, and I am happy to say that his dog will be taken to a very lovely no-kill animal shelter where hopefully he'll find healing and the love of a new home.

~ Seeker of Justice

Wilson handed the evidence envelope over to the officer first on scene then stood scratching his head as he perused the body, "I gotta say, Hardwick, I'm finding it hard to hate this woman."

"Then hate the actions," Hardwick replied, pointing to the black man lying face up on the warped tile floor.

"Yeah, which one: the one where she beat the crap out of a spousal and animal abuser or the one where she rescued the dog?" Wilson quipped sarcastically. Hardwick glanced up from the body and

75

speared him with a look that told him his sarcasm wasn't welcomed.

"The one where we know she's not done yet and she wants us to know it; the one where she's now rubbing it in our faces instead of killing quietly—"

"I got it!"

"Good! Now, these marks confirm that the victim was tased in the chest, likely rendering him vulnerable—"

"Then what, a woman of unknown age and size manages to wrench the belt from his hand and beat the crap out of him?" Wilson retorted, finding it difficult to keep the sarcasm from his tone. He hated that he was flung into the middle of another serial killer case. Mainly because he dreaded that it could end like the Christian Price case. He looked up to Hardwick, his partner now for three years, but he also worried over what the Price case had taken out of him; worried that he was close to burning out, making his mental acuity less than up to the task of catching another serial psychopath.

"That's what the bruising suggests, and the belt lying next to the body suggests. Of course, the belt could've just been lying around somewhere already, so no wrenching required."

"Yeah, so she tases him then has the time to locate his belt…what's the cause of death? Other than bruising from the belt beating, I'm not seeing petechiae or bruising to suggest strangulation, no blood, nor anything to suggest blunt force trauma—"

"You mean belt marks covering his body isn't blunt force enough for you?" It was Hardwick's turn to turn up the sarcasm, but he quickly reigned himself in, forcing himself to focus.

"No, smart ass, I mean lumps like being whacked over the head with a hammer. Unless you're suggesting that belting a person this size can kill them. Could the taser have killed him?"

"I'm assuming that's hypothetical, since we won't know anything definitive until the medical examiner gets him on her table."

"Detective Hardwick, Detective Wilson, you aren't going to like this," a uniformed officer stated soberly, handing Hardwick a slip of paper. He passed it to Wilson then turned back to the officer.

"Contact the desk officer. Have him pass the details on to Harding and Cortez. We'll meet them there as soon as we've wrapped up here."

Wilson handed the slip of paper back to the officer and then looked at Hardwick, "you really think we've got another one, by this killer, based on an address on a piece of paper?"

Hardwick shook his head, "address equals crime scene or the officer wouldn't have bothered us with it. You know that, Wilson. Whether it's connected to this case or not…we'll know more when we get there. The thing banging through my head right now is why our killer has suddenly started leaving little love notes at the scene of her kills. If she's been killing these last three years, as she suggested, why hasn't a note turned up prior? Why now?"

"She said it, remember? That's why she mailed us her incomplete manuscript. She's not done yet and she wants us to know who she is…so…the notes are a cry for help? She wants to get caught? She's tired of not getting credit for her kills? Pick any number of clichéd reasons."

Hardwick pursed his lips and huffed heavily from his nostrils, then started shaking his head, "I think it's more that all of this started again when she began writing her purported memoirs. Maybe she'd taken out those who'd caused her harm, then stopped and went on with her life. When she started to recount her actions in writing, something in her snapped, maybe? I don't know…" he continued, kneeling to stare at the man's face intently. Seeing nothing, he stood and started for the front door. Stopping briefly by a side table, he snatched up a photo. "Let's go. We'll follow up with the medical examiner later. We've got another crime scene to visit."

78

He stopped just outside, "Officer."

"Yes, detective." A young, eager boy in uniform turned quickly from his conversation with another officer.

"I need you to do some research for me. Get your sergeant to clear it with me, if needed."

"Yes, sir. What do you need me to do?"

"You're going to track down a Pitbull." He handed over the picture of a young woman kneeling next to her brown bull terrier, a smile on her face that had likely been absent for too long after she'd met and married her husband, now dead. Would that smile return now that the abuse was over? He could hope it did, for her sake. That made him want to laud this current killer. Unlike Price, whose twisted sense of justice caused the cruel deaths of too many, this woman was bringing peace and security back into the lives of those who'd suffered at the hands of a batterer.

"Why do we need to find the dog?" Wilson queried as they climbed into their Dodge Charger. "Trying to reunite mother and pet? Think it'll make her heal faster?"

"Wish I'd thought of that," Hardwick confessed, pursing his lips. "Mainly I was hoping that if we find where the dog was dropped off, the facility will have surveillance cameras that we can use to identify our killer."

"That would make my millennium and is certainly probable since cameras are everywhere nowadays."

"Yeah, but it still hasn't made the apprehension of all criminals easy, nor has it made our jobs a piece of cake either."

Wilson snorted without humor, "yeah, I know. Too many people releasing doctored or incomplete footage on social media sites causing haters to hate more and closing doors that hinder our investigation efforts…" he trailed off, knowing it was a topic that Hardwick preferred to avoid. Hardwick was of the opinion that it didn't matter what obstacles were thrown in their path, it was their job to jump and dodge them to close a case. It was a stance that Wilson admired.

As they pulled up to the scene of the next murder, both men's brows knitted in concern. The plastic evidence bag being carried by a uniform showed the evidence easily identifiable as a piece of paper with scripted text on it, and though they couldn't read the words, both knew that it was likely a continued reflection written by their killer. She was rapidly moving from serial killer to spree killer and that had them growing exceedingly concerned.

Hardwick threw the car into park and leapt out, sprinting toward the officer, "let me see that!" he called. The officer stopped and handed over the bag.

"Don't open that, sir. Chain of command—"

"I know. I just want to give it a read through…" he trailed off as he lifted the bag and scanned the contents.

"What's it say?" Wilson queried, leaning around the side of his partner to try to read the letter also. Hardwick handed it over and headed toward the house, his shoulders slumped. Wilson watched his partner and drew in a deep breath before reading the letter.

The infestation is so much worse than I could even have imagined. The sickness in these souls that cause them to lash out at those for whom they've professed an unwavering love. Are they just words then? Do they hold any meaning at all or are they merely platitudes uttered by narcissists to gain control over the unwitting.

If you must know, I hadn't meant to kill again this night. Was actually exhausted and looking forward to a nice cup of hot tea and my leftover Stroganoff, but as I was wending my way through the ever-crowding neighborhoods of Atlanta, my glance fell upon the scene through a front window, of a man engaged in an act of brutality. Is it so hard to simply say that the food prepared for dinner is in need of salt? Must the plate be lifted and slammed atop the head of the one who so obviously made an effort to please?

My heart was pounding in sadness as I pulled alongside the curb and watched, yet again, as a woman cowered beneath the blows of her significant other before he stormed from the house, abandoning her in a battered condition.

I could only call for an ambulance and was pleased that it arrived quickly and took her away to be tended while I whiled away the time awaiting the return of the man who caused the need for medical assistance in the first place. By the time I concluded my business with him, no medical assistance would save his soul, which I damned to Hell. Something I plan to do with as many as able before justice and I meet.

~ Seeker of Justice

Wilson shivered involuntarily as he handed the evidence bag back to the officer, "Get on with dispatch. See if they can't obtain the call for the ambulance. Have the recording and transcript sent over to Captain Parsons. Also, have the front desk contact Harding and Cortez. Since we're here ahead of them, there's no need for them to come. We'll meet up with them back at the precinct." The officer nodded and then Wilson headed into the house to join his partner.

"The ambulance—" Hardwick started thoughtfully.

"I'm already on it," Wilson interjected, and Hardwick nodded.

"Thanks. Her words—"

"Affected me too, yeah. So much sadness and hostility."

"I can't help but wonder how heinous the acts were against this woman that she's now driven to rid the world of abusive people. It's becoming almost like a compulsion. It makes me shiver to think, that had she written more about her abuse in her memoirs—"

"Worried that she'll develop a taste for it and just start killing randomly? No more justifications?"

"She's killed two men in one night—"

"That we know of."

"Right," Hardwick concurred, "and who's to say what might nudge her that much closer to becoming a random killer. No abuse needed. Just look at her cross-eyed and she pulls out a gun and starts blasting. A regular modern-day Jesse James."

"We know the pathology of abuse doesn't play a roll in creating a killer—"

"Maybe not, but it certainly gives a killer their excuse. And her journal entry mentioned an abusive mom and husband."

"We're done in the kitchen," the police photographer stated as she moved past the two detectives. The medical examiner was closing her bag when Hardwick and Wilson entered.

"I know this is going to sound cliché, but this really is a first in my book," she said without looking up. "The perpetrator must have emptied every cupboard of every dish to cause this level of chaos. And based on the contusions covering nearly every inch of his body, that I can currently see, and many of which I'll discover when I get him on my slab, he—"

"She," Wilson corrected.

"She? Wow," Dr. Monica Percival exclaimed, shaking her head. She stood to face the detectives. "This is one angry she. Anyway, she either used one dish to land repeated blows then threw the remaining dishes around the kitchen—"

"Or she beat him with each and every one of them," Hardwick concluded.

"Yeah, which is really odd, considering he was likely already bleeding out from the cuts from the broken ceramic plates. And since the blood is pooled around the head more than spattered all over the place, I'd say he was bleeding out from what looks to me to be a rather deliberate slice along the carotid, while she went to town on him—beating him with everything she could get her hands on. Talk about overkill. All of this is, of course, speculation."

"Any sign that he was downed using a taser to the chest?" Hardwick asked, his gaze taking in the swollen beaten face of a man who just a few hours earlier had done the same to his live-in girlfriend or spouse.

Dr. Percival shook her head, "I haven't examined him that fully as yet," she said, then knelt carefully beside the victim. She unclasped her bag and reached inside, retrieving a clean pair of nitrile gloves, then began to unbutton the victim's flannel shirt. Meanwhile, Hardwick let his gaze move around the room, "Where are Harding and Cortez? I thought they'd be here before us."

"Since we arrived first, I told the officer to cancel their call; for them to head on back to the precinct," Wilson offered before turning his attention back to Dr. Percival. "Any injection sites?" he asked.

"Not that I can visually detect through the damages, and I won't know if he was injected with anything until we run a tox screen. There are signs of blunt force trauma to the side of his head," she continued, opening his shirt to expose his chest, "but I don't know if that's the cause of death, the blow that took him down, or if it's just one of the blows inflicted on his way down. He's in really bad shape." She leaned over to inspect his chest, moving aside the chest hairs with her gloved fingertips. "Too thick," she muttered, sitting back on her haunches. "Can't see anything through the chest hair, but if he was tased here—or anywhere else on his body—it'll be in my report." She

85

pulled off her gloves and shoved them into her bag, then stood again. "You know, I'm surprised that neither of you mentioned the smell of booze, although admittedly," she sniffed the air, "it has dissipated a bit since I arrived. Fairly reeked in here."

"Drunk, I take it?" Hardwick asked, sniffing the air also.

"Stinking."

"Would probably explain how she managed to do all of this damage to him—"

"With no noticeable signs of defense," Dr. Percival interjected. "Well, detectives. I've had a busy night and me and my colleagues are in for a long haul with the number of bodies coming in, and not all from your killer."

"We get it—we'll get the results when we get the results," Wilson interpreted correctly.

"Sorry fellas. We'll do our best, as always, to get them to you before anything goes to trial."

"Gotta catch our killer first," Hardwick muttered.

"Then we've got plenty of time…" Dr. Percival stopped when she realized how that sounded. "I didn't mean—"

86

"No worries, doctor. We know it takes time to catch a killer—most times."

Dr. Percival nodded solemnly, "Let the undertaker know when he can come in and remove the body, will ya?"

"Sure."

She left the two detectives alone to peruse the mess around them. Hardwick pulled over one of the dining room chairs and settled onto it, rubbing his face as he released sigh after sigh. He lifted his head to look at the white male, his body blacker and bluer than white from the repeated blows.

"There are a few things that we know now that we didn't know before," he said thoughtfully. "First, she's attacking these men in the manner in which they attacked their victims—if the letters she's penning are an indicator—which means she's witnessing the assaults. Second, she's taking the time to pen her notes after each assault, which means she's driving around with a legal tablet and ink pen looking for victims. Finally, she's not settled on a single MO, she's all over the map. This makes six kills in three years—

"That we know of."

"All killed in different ways, and the time between kills is accelerating."

"I'd say," Wilson snorted. "Four in three years and now two in one night. That's more than just acceleration, that's a freaking rocket launch. To make it more disturbing, we also know that she's forensically knowledgeable, to a point."

"In what way?"

"Gloves. She's got to be wearing gloves, unless you think forensics is going to find prints at either of these scenes."

"That's a huge assumptive leap. What made you jump there?"

"Gut feeling I've got that she wouldn't screw up by not wearing gloves. If she were dumb enough to leave prints at any of those four earlier kills, despite differing MOs, do you not think forensics would've found them? I don't know. I just get the feeling she isn't that stupid. Maybe it's the way she writes—"

"I don't want to attribute her with an overabundance of intelligence just yet, Wilson. But I was thinking something similar," Hardwick interjected. "Her calm after the storm. She kills these men then remorselessly returns to her vehicle, pens florid prose, returns to the scene of her brutality, and places the paper near her own victim."

"Florid? More like deranged. And, if uniforms are correct, she does it all without being seen by any neighbors."

"Yeah, that doesn't surprise me since she's assaulting these people at night when most are too busy watching television or are already asleep."

"It's going to be an exercise in futility to have forensics check the paper for fingerprints."

"Yeah, I can't envision she's that careless, and since the paper is standard legal paper that can be purchased anywhere...no, they'll do their due diligence and test the paper, but they won't find anything."

"Where to now? Unless you think we'll serve any purpose hanging around here any longer."

"No, we have to use our time as wisely as able. Uniforms have collected what they can. We've done our part searching the scene best we can, but since we know that this was a targeted kill by a person most likely unknown to the victim, searching the house for further clues will be a waste of our limited time. We call it a night and tomorrow hope that the uniforms have found additional information in the cold case files that will assist in identifying this killer. More importantly, we keep our fingers crossed that the call for the ambulance didn't come from a burner phone."

Chapter seven

The following morning

"Mom, it's time to get up. I let you sleep a few minutes longer because you got home so late again…where are you going and why are you getting home so late at night…" the chattering from her now seventeen-year-old Katie seemed endless and Bethany had to close her eyes and draw in deep breaths to remain calm.

Her daughter was a cheery morning person, while Bethany was more of a mid-morning, need a cup of coffee to get her cheer on type of person; however, she'd made a vow to herself, soon after Shane's death, that she would never lose her temper with her daughters over what was obviously a personality trait and especially one that was so joyous in nature, not when she'd prayed incessantly that they heal and find genuine joy and a passion for living. The loss of their father and then Shane's abuse for much of their lives was more than any child should have to endure.

It was especially important since being tired and irritable was all on her and her late-night forays for justice. It didn't help that her headaches still plagued her, and one was threatening again now.

Jessica, now eighteen, sauntered into the room and flopped onto the edge of her bed. She, like her mother, wasn't a morning person. Bethany eyed the cup of coffee in her daughter's hand suspiciously.

"That coffee sure does smell good. Is that for me?" Bethany asked, feigning excessive sleepiness, when in fact Katie's jabbering more than assured that she was fully awake.

"Not on your life. You want coffee? Get out of bed like I had to do," Jessica teased.

"You're heartless!"

"Daggum straight."

Bethany closed her eyes again and pretended to snore. "Mom, we promised the twins a birthday to remember, and if we're going to make that happen, you need to get a move on."

"Oh, there's nothing like being harangued and chastised by your two oldest daughters first thing in the morning," Bethany grumbled good naturedly.

"Well, if you'd been up at seven when you said you'd be up, we wouldn't have to be either of those things," Jessica berated lightly.

Bethany glanced at the time on her Fitbit, "You are aware that it's only seven fifteen, right? Your sister ensured that I didn't get much past our arranged time."

"Daggum right I did," Katie preened proudly.

Bethany grinned. For a seventeen-year-old, she often behaved more like a seven-year-old. She wondered if it wasn't because she'd only been allowed to be a real child these past few years and was simply playing catch up. Jessica, on the other hand, as the eldest, tended to be far more mature than her age would suggest. Though only a year older than Katie, the trials in their young lives had aged Jessica far greater. Bethany tried desperately to let them grow and develop into who they were going to be without smothering them or sheltering them too tightly.

She soaked in their love in an attempt to help herself heal, but for her it was slow-going. Her scars went far deeper. She shook herself mentally, hurling away the thoughts from the past, but they never stayed gone long. "Are the twins still sleeping?"

"You know that an atom bomb couldn't wake those two on a weekend. At least not before eight a.m., which might I remind you will be upon us in less than forty-five minutes, and we made a deal to be out the door and on our way no later than eight thirty a.m. so we could grab breakfast—"

"Are you certain I'm the mom in this house?" Bethany interrupted with a laugh.

Jessica let out a loud laugh but quickly covered her mouth the stifle it. To her tired fogged brain, Bethany's mind immediately jumped to the many times they all would have to stifle their laughter to ensure they didn't wake Shane from his sleep, not that they realized until much later, that waking him would take far more than peals of laughter since he drank himself into a stupor each morning upon arriving home from work.

Bethany hadn't even known he was an alcoholic nor a smoker because he generally snuck into the back yard to smoke and imbibe before she and the girls were awake and would stumble to bed and fall asleep just before she crawled out of bed to start her day.

During their many phone calls, prior to meeting for the first time, she'd repeatedly told him that she wasn't interested in getting involved with a smoker or drinker and he'd assured her that he didn't do either.

Nearly four years into their marriage, Bethany found a pack of cigarettes hidden behind the medicine cabinet in the old bathroom off the back porch and a bottle of vodka behind Shane's desk in the computer room. She hadn't gone looking but was doing one of her frenzied cleanings. Something she did when particularly stressed. Finding those things hadn't helped her stress level at all and when Shane emerged from the bedroom to get ready for work, she lost all sense of care for her safety and confronted him.

"All these years, and even before we got married, you swore to me that you didn't drink or smoke. You knew how I felt about this stuff; knew I never would have married you…" The grin that split his lips was so malevolent that it ceased her tirade. He *had* known, which is why he'd kept it secret.

Soon after he left for work that evening, she called his stepmother. His parents lived in California, so they didn't have the closest relationship; had visited only once. Bethany never felt particularly close to them and had felt like she was watching his family from the outside for all the warmth and welcome they extended to her. She knew it was because Shane had deigned to marry a woman with children—four of them at that.

Admittedly, it was easy to get overlooked on their visit. With Shane's eight siblings, their spouses and dozens of kids jammed inside the small house in Inglewood, chaos was the order of the day when they'd arrived, so she spent the entire visit settled on the outskirts of that chaos tending to her children, who'd been equally ignored in the mayhem. She'd been contented enough to do so. It hadn't cultivated a warm relationship with his parents though.

Still, if anyone was going to be able to give her answers, she hoped it would be Shane's stepmother. She'd taken two pieces of information away from their abbreviated conversation, neither of which left her feeling safe or secure: that Shane had been drinking like a sailor and smoking like a chimney since the age of nine and, even more alarming, she perceived him to have a "dark soul". After revealing that last particular tidbit in a voice that tremored in dread, she'd hung up, as if speaking about her stepson in such a manner would unleash the hounds of Hell upon her. She wracked her brain, pulling recollections from that brief stay in California and realized then that she had not been the only person to sit on the fringes of the chaos. Shane's stepmom had also. She'd stayed well away from Shane and his siblings as they reveled. The act had been lost on her then. Perhaps in her mind, she simply thought that the stepmom felt as many did—an outsider that didn't really belong at family gatherings.

Now, she knew better and that brief, two-word description and the knowledge that she'd married a raging alcoholic explained so much: the verbal threats, the physical abuse, the attempts to run her over with his car because he thought it was funny, the mercurial temperament…it was also then that she knew she and her daughters had to get away, that they were in far more danger than she ever realized before.

Early one morning, right after Shane fell asleep, she rounded up the girls and headed for the car. She didn't know where she was going, but she knew she had to get out. The devil must have been whispering in his ear that morning because Shane—who usually couldn't be woken easily, once asleep—came tearing out after her and wrenched Tanya from her grasp.

"Come back inside or I swear to God, I'll kill her," he hissed close to Bethany's face.

"Give me my daughter! Now, Shane!"

"Give me the car keys and get back inside," he snarled, his dark eyes nearly black with rage. Bethany was shaking in fear and infuriation. The pleading cries from her daughters were deafening her, breaking her heart into tiny pieces. They were scared; she was terrified.

Yet, as petrified as she was, it would be years more of threats and abuse, living in fear that he'd kill her or one of her precious babies, before she gained the courage to eliminate him from their lives, but during that time, her terror intensified to where the slightest noise made by her daughters while Shane was sleeping made her quiver and she'd whisper at them to cover their mouth, so they didn't laugh too loud, or shushed them if they spoke too loudly. She hated herself for imposing such restrictions on their joy.

"Mom, are you okay?" Jessica asked softly. Katie, who'd been prattling on, heard her sister's tone and quickly moved to settle on the other side of the bed. Both girls took one of their mom's hands, squeezing it in comfort.

"I was just worried," Bethany croaked, "that our laughing might wake the twins—"

"Mom, this is us you're talking to remember?" Jessica interrupted. "You went white as a sheet."

"Did I?"

"It's been years, mom," Katie added. "You don't have to be afraid anymore. None of us do. He died, remember? He can't hurt—"

"I know, sweetheart. I know." Bethany drew in a deep breath, threw back her blankets, swung her feet out over Jessica's head and planted them firmly onto the cool tile floor, slapping her thighs determinedly, "And since I'm not about to make this day about past traumas, I'm getting up to take a quick shower before we haul those twins out of bed and head out the door. We've been planning this day for six months and there ain't nothing going to spoil their birthday."

"Mom, are you ever going to look for a therapist?" Jessica asked, grabbing her mom's hand again and holding it tight. Katie grabbed her other hand, mimicking Jessica's actions.

"You both know that I don't hold to talking to strangers about my personal life. I find catharsis in my writing."

"Keeping a journal is good, mom, but talking it through with someone is better," Katie interjected. "If you didn't believe in that then why are you paying for me and Jessica to see one?"

97

"Because you two don't have a qualm about talking to a therapist and I want what's best for you both. I'm just cut from a different cloth."

"Journaling is cathartic. Our therapist said so, but is it enough for you? We know that you put a lot of your life into your books too, but if those things were good enough, would you still be struggling so much after all this time? I covered my mouth to keep from waking the twins, but your thoughts immediately jumped to Shane, right? We saw your face, mom, so don't try to deny it."

Bethany nodded, "We had to keep quiet for so many years, so when I saw you stifle yourself…it was hard for me to see. I'm working on not allowing things to trigger me, but…" Bethany stopped speaking. She closed her eyes, and drew in deep, relaxing breaths. "I've relied on breathing and writing for a long time, but since I'm not seeing the results that we'd all like to see, I promise that I'll start looking for a therapist first thing tomorrow…oh wait, tomorrow is Sunday and I have jobs on Monday to Wednesday, but definitely Thursday. Fair enough?"

Jessica and Katie wrapped their arms around their mom's neck, "Fair enough," they both said simultaneously.

"Good, then do you think maybe I can take a really quick shower so we can start the celebrations?"

"Yep, you're free to go now. Therapy session terminated at…" Jessica paused, glancing at her watch, "07:22".

Bethany laughed, "Smart butt. Are you guys ready to go?"

"We've been ready since six thirty," Katie laughed, "so you better get a move on."

"Do you think one of you could make me a cup of coffee to go? I really could use one."

"I'll get you one, mom," Jessica offered.

"And I'll get the twins up and light a fire under them. They have to get ready too."

"Appreciate it," Bethany took a deep breath, closed the bathroom door behind her, then turned and started the shower running. As soon as she stepped into the tub, she turned her face into the warm spray, allowing it to wash away the tears streaming down her cheeks, and to soothe her weary soul.

Chapter eight

"Nothing? We've got nothing?" Hardwick forced himself to remain seated before the captain's desk, but his mind, racing in disbelief, made it difficult.

"Not one cold case fit our killer? No similarities? *Nada?*" Cortez asked, incredulously.

"The uniforms and I went back years and there were no deaths of individuals who died in a similar manner in which they were abusing their victims. Not one. Those with an abusive history were either murdered by their spouse or someone known to the family, gang affiliated, by natural causes or accidental."

"All that tells us is that she only just started killing in a similar fashion to the abuse," Hardwick said in a tone that showed how unhappy he was about that particular development.

"Which helps us not a whit," Harding mumbled grumpily.

"What about cases involving death by chemical fumes, ruled accidental?" Hardwick asked.

"We're still working through the files. We started with unsolved. Haven't moved on to those ruled accidental."

"Not likely to hit the jackpot though, are we?" Wilson interjected thoughtfully. "I was thinking about it, and I personally know of three cases in recent months where an older person died because they mixed chemicals, so imagine how many potentials there could be, especially with so many baby boomers hitting old age in the last decade."

"Well, I can't even begin to guess how many deaths are as a result of chemical fumes each year, but we'll know once the detectives finish sorting through the computer files. Maybe we'll get lucky."

"I know that I swore off swearing for my baby's sake, but I'll be daggumed if I don't want to let loose some choice words that would melt the ears off a priest," Harding growled through clenched teeth.

"Oh, you won't be able to contain yourself in a few more seconds, because the news doesn't get better," the captain intoned as he tossed a folder across to Hardwick.

Hardwick opened the folder hesitantly, then slapped it back onto the desk, his efforts to remain calm and in control of his emotions abandoned, "Damn it all to Hell and back," he yelled, pacing in agitation.

"What? What's happened?" Wilson asked, snatching up the folder. Whatever got far enough under Hardwick's skin to cause him to lose control was never good. He scanned the contents of the folder and quickly passed it to Cortez, "I wouldn't show that to Harding, if I were you, because if it set Hardwick to cursing a blue streak, you can only imagine what'll happen to him," Wilson quipped without humor. He sat rubbing his face, drawing in deep breaths to maintain his own composure.

"I don't fucking believe this," Cortez muttered, then began swearing in his native tongue. He clenched the folder so tight that Harding had to yank at it repeatedly to try to get his grip to loosen, "Let go, you SOB."

"Wilson's right, *jefe*, you don't want to—"

"Give it here, you asshole!" Harding snapped, yanking so hard that he nearly toppled from his chair when Cortez released it suddenly. He opened the folder then just as quickly hurled it across the room.

He stood abruptly, his lips clenched tight, his head shaking, "I just…I…I can't…I need some air," he concluded, storming from the captain's office.

The captain remained still, leaning back in his chair, watching each of his detectives thoughtfully. Each were seasoned veterans, with the exception of Wilson, but each appeared on the verge of a mental breakdown. Yes, the news hadn't been what they were hoping for, but their reaction to it had been more than he'd anticipated. He could only surmise that each man was still reeling from the Price case; each still dealing with the demons that had cost the lives of too many women;

each still blaming themselves for their parts in not catching him fast enough.

He'd nearly lost Hardwick after that case but had convinced him that he'd done everything humanly possible to bring that serial killer to justice. They'd made a pact to do more to prevent something like that happening again in future, but the future hadn't been far enough away to enact new policies and procedures; too soon for them to be confronted with another determined killer.

"At least we haven't had another death in a few days," Wilson muttered. "Maybe her spree was short lived, or maybe after the beating she gave her last victim, she lost her taste—"

"You and I both know that her letters at the scene don't reflect that. She said she'd continue until she was caught," Hardwick ground out.

"Yeah, but she could have written that when fueled by the adrenaline of the kill, right?"

Hardwick just closed his eyes and settled back onto his chair, the one thing in the folder that he didn't want to read reverberating about in his head like a fiery pinball: burner phone, which meant that all they got from the trace was a general location, near the house of the victim for whom she'd called the ambulance. Nothing more because it wasn't registered to an individual.

"What about the recorded call? Has that been sent over yet?" Hardwick asked.

The captain pulled up a file from his computer, "I was hoping you wouldn't ask that," he muttered, then hit play. The clip was exceptionally abbreviated; the caller stating: *Ambulancia de Novecientos setenta y cinco Oak street.*

"That's it?" "She's Spanish?" Wilson and Hardwick asked simultaneously.

"No, she's not Spanish," Cortez piped up. "Definitely a *Gringa*. Likely used Google translate to hear how to pronounce the address before calling. Picked it up fast though. Gotta give her kudos for that. Her enunciation was near flawless, but I could tell," he concluded smugly.

"To what end?" The captain asked.

"Throw us off the track, obviously," Cortez sneered.

"Yeah, and in addition to the accent, it's obvious that she deepened her voice too," Hardwick added. "All because she likely knew we'd do a voice print analysis if we ever linked her to the killings and brought her in to interview."

"Shit, that's slick," Wilson murmured, unable to keep the admiration from his tone. "Talk about quick thinking. Most people wouldn't think to disguise their voice when calling 911 for assistance."

"Most people don't generally plan to commit murder soon after," Hardwick added, his tone less appreciative.

"So, basically this is useless," the captain added, "which is why I wasn't going to play it. Didn't think it would lead anywhere, but it did help confirm my suspicions that she was faking the Spanish accent…anyway, let's move—."

"Not useless, Captain," Cortez interposed. "It removes a specific demographic from the suspect pool: Hispanic females. When we collect sufficient data to start narrowing down our suspect pool, at least."

"True enough. Any word back from the lab about fingerprints or from the coroner, or…anything else to go on at all?" Wilson asked the captain, his tone imploring.

"Nothing yet, and before you ask: no camera footage from anywhere around the area of the deaths because there are either no cameras, being as it's a residential zone, or they're all nonfunctioning."

"Nonfunctioning, my ass," Cortez snapped. "We all know what happens to security cameras around Atlanta."

"Yeah," Harding snapped, having returned from a very short walk-it-off session, "they get covered, painted, unplugged, or yanked out of the wall by taggers, gang members, thieves, or kids just up to no good, just like any other city. I'll give any of you a hundred dollars if you can find a working camera within a ten-mile radius of where those crimes were committed. Oh, and let's not forget that COVID had everybody masking up which gave thieves and villains another way to beat security—those not already covering their faces, anyway, so even if you were to find a working camera, it's not likely you'll get an ident off it, unless they happen to be wearing a mask with their name stitched on it," he concluded, plopping down on his chair.

"You good, *jefe*?" Cortez asked softly.

Harding shook his head, "I'm present and accounted for. That's the best you're getting right now. Did I miss any more bombshells?"

"I'll let Cortez fill you in after we're done here. In the meantime, chill out, okay?" the captain snapped lightly. "Residential zones don't usually have security cameras, which is what I said, so all this jabbering over broken or vandalized systems isn't productive."

"Have we sent officers around to see if anyone has a Ring camera..."

"Already done," the captain muttered, then wiped a hand along his face. "Only two people at the

106

second crime scene and they weren't facing the residence where the murder took place. As for the first murder location, no doorbell cameras at all."

"Is she fucking planning things this way?" Harding snarled.

"We know that isn't likely, so don't go there," Cortez said, trying to reign in his partner's temper.

"What about footage from the no-kill shelters? Tell me there was footage of a woman bringing in a Pitbull—"

The captain was shaking his head, so Wilson stopped talking. "Apparently, since theft isn't a concern, they don't feel the need for a security camera," the captain concluded, then sighed heavily. "This woman's last two kills happened just a week ago, but it may as well have been as old as her first four kills, with as little evidence obtained thus far. People have a preconceived notion that chasing down bad guys is an easy thing. What many don't realize is that a lot of the time, catching a criminal comes down to their carelessness. Asininely leaving fingerprints at the scene or bragging about it on social media; committing the crime in front of eyewitnesses, someone with a cellphone camera, or a working security camera. Or just a routine traffic stop. Not catching this killer quickly isn't something we need to hang our head over. We haven't gotten the full picture yet—"

"The remaining results from the lab or the coroner," Harding concluded.

"Right. And if there's nothing there, then we wait—"

"Until she kills again and then pray hard that one of your scenarios help us bring her to justice," Wilson chimed in.

"I know that we're all still hurting from our perceived mistakes in the Christian Price case—"

"There was nothing perceived about our cockups, captain," Hardwick interjected harshly. "We royally screwed up in ways that made us look like rookies. Shit, we even had our rookies screw up."

"I'm aware of our shortcomings on that case, Hardwick, but I'm also aware that this case does not mirror that one in any way, shape, or form."

"Other than her intelligence," Hardwick murmured, suddenly thoughtful. "It's easy to see it in her writing, just as it was easy to perceive in the way Price spoke."

"I thought we agreed that the way she wrote was a little more than twisted," Wilson asserted.

"No, I described it as florid prose, you said it was deranged."

"And I stand by that, so what's your point? Because if you're going to say that she's not stupid, that isn't going to go a long way in boosting our confidence any. Stupid would be more likely to screw up, intelligent…don't go there."

Hardwick nodded thoughtfully, "I get you, I do, but this woman isn't stupid. At least not in the way that would work well in our favor. She's well written which likely means educated, maybe a writer."

"A novelist?" Cortez interjected, sitting forward in his seat, his eyes lit in anticipation of whatever revelation Hardwick was working toward.

"Or a news columnist, or a blogger, or…shit…any number of occupations in which writing would be an essential on a resume," Hardwick sighed heavily. "Without any additional bodies, currently, and since we're stuck awaiting results, what harm is there in doing a little research?"

"What kind of research?"

"Think back over her letters? What age would you peg her to be?"

"Mature, definitely," Wilson commented. "Late thirties, early forties."

"I concur," Hardwick replied, nodding. "We also know that she would have suffered at the hands of a spouse."

109

"And, based on her incomplete memoirs, she was abused by her mom growing up also," Cortez added.

"Okay, okay, so then, we break up our research into…Harding, you search for female novelists in their late thirties, early forties. Wilson, you start finding bloggers. Cortez, digital and print news. Same age parameters. Atlanta proper. I'll start scanning social media sites. Make a note of everyone who fits the bill. We'll whittle it down from there by deep diving into their backgrounds: personal webpages, interviews, or any other speaking engagements in which they discuss abuse as a part of their childhood or an abusive partner. Cross-reference that with the dates in which our killer would have been abused. Am I missing anything?"

"Yeah, that she's a *gringa*," Cortez added.

"Right, anything else?"

"Yeah, a huge something and I've got to say it. What if she's not from here? What if she moved here after her first four kills. Ran from her past. A lot of people run from the ghosts of their past. It may be why we didn't catch her, because she didn't kill those first four here in Atlanta."

Hardwick nodded, his lips pursed thoughtfully, "that's true, Wilson, but we have to start somewhere, with some parameters in place. We can't identify every female novelist in the U.S., or even just in Georgia, or

110

we'd be buried in so much information that we'd never dig our way out. We set our parameters in doable increments. If nothing turns up, and we still feel it's worth continuing along these veins, we'll open the search grid and put uniforms on it. Fair enough?"

Wilson nodded, "fair enough."

Captain Parsons watched the exchange and felt a surge of relief seeing his lead detective's mind back at work. For a long time, he truly felt as if it may have been better to just let Hardwick retire, but something held him back from accepting that resignation. Watching his mind work now gave him renewed hope he'd made the right call. "We'll still end up putting uniforms on it," he interjected.

"Because she's not done yet," Cortez whispered.

The captain nodded, "And we'll need you four out there tracking her down when she kills again."

"I'd rather you'd used the word *if*," Wilson groaned.

"I think we all know that she's not done yet," the captain sighed heavily.

"Then we better get started before someone triggers her into killing again," Hardwick stated firmly.

Chapter nine

"Hey, mom, how was work?" Jessica asked on her way out of the bathroom.

"Nice. You off to work?" Bethany asked, peeling off her booties and coveralls. She hung them on the peg on the back of the bathroom door and then headed for the kitchen to make dinner.

"No, night classes. I only work on the weekends, Mom, you know that."

"Oh yeah, right. You sure you aren't pushing yourself too hard, sweetheart? You'll be off to University in the fall, so there ain't no cause for you to be taking college courses at night too. That, and working part time on the weekends…you're going to burn yourself out. Katie too."

"It's okay, mom," she yelled from her bedroom. "Katie and I are doing what we have to do so we can get a leg up. Taking classes now means I'll graduate University sooner. Same with Katie. We graduate faster, we get a good paying job faster. That'll take some of the financial strain off your back. You still have the twins to support for a few more years. You don't need to be using all that insurance money to support us too. If we need to slow down, or if we get too tired, we'll take a break from the night classes. We've both got finals this week, so there'll be a short break before the next classes start."

"Heard and understood. You feeling good about the finals?" Bethany shouted from the kitchen. This was par for the course in their home now, calling out in conversation no matter where in the house they were. They'd spent so much time in silence or whispering, that it was as if they'd all made the same vow never to be quiet again.

"Yep. Confidence is my middle name."

Bethany laughed. She loved that both of her daughters had chosen a field of study in the mental health profession. Jessica was working towards becoming a Psychiatrist and Katie planned to be a Clinical Psychologist. "Have you eaten?"

"No time. I was helping the twins finish up their homework, so I'm running late. I'll grab something on my way."

"Where's are the twins? And Katie?"

"Mom, I gotta go or I won't be able to grab food. Katie left for class about half an hour ago and the twins went down the street to Angela's house. Said they'd be back in a few. I'll see you later tonight. Bye."

"Love you."

"Love you too."

The house fell silent and Bethany's plans to make dinner turned into a sandwich for herself. She went into the computer room and turned on her laptop.

After doing a quick check of her budget and entering receipts onto her spreadsheet, she typed in the web address for the Fort Refuge chat room. It was a place recommended to her by a therapist during an introductory session, when she'd explained that she wasn't comfortable yet talking to someone one-on-one, plus she admitted that she was already spending a fortune for her daughters' therapy sessions. It had turned out to be good for her since she could step into the chat whenever she was feeling the need to post something and have like-minded individuals respond. Depending on the day she had and her level of stress, she could choose to discuss her PTSD or simply have an innocuous conversation about kittens and puppies.

This evening, it was her PTSD. Even though she'd had a decent day at work, painting the interiors of a new set of houses going up in the neighboring town, the drive home provided too many opportunities for her mind to wander or to witness too many people hurting one another. It always left her feeling anxious even though she did her best to put on a happy face when entering the house.

She found it odd that the home that she'd purchased prior to marrying Shane had been both home

114

to joy and laughter and also crying and misery. Many people she'd spoken to in her chat sessions wondered why she hadn't sold the house and moved somewhere else because they, themselves, would feel continually triggered if they'd remained in a home in which they'd been abused.

Admittedly, that had been an issue for her for a while after killing Shane, but it had slowly dissipated because she'd remind herself constantly that the home was hers, purchased with her hard-earned dollars; that Shane was dead and she'd been the one brave enough to kill him; and Shane had died away from that house, so it wasn't tainted with memories of his corpse lying on the floor somewhere.

No, her biggest triggers weren't of the home she occupied, happily, with her four daughters, rather those events which happened when she left to go to work. She immediately started a chat about a couple she spotted in a QuikTrip parking lot while stopped at a red light. Her first instinct had been to pull in and insert herself between the recoiling woman and the much larger muscle-bound jerk who was yelling at her. The battle to intervene was nearly decided when she saw him slap her across the face. When the light turned green, she turned into the parking lot, but when she noticed a cop car approaching from the other direction, she did a U-turn and headed back onto the main road. Seeing the officer move to assist provided a sense of relief. She was still rattled, but relieved.

It set me back years as I struggled to overcome my own fears over the assaults I'd endured in defense of my daughters, and before that, the mental and verbal abuse that my mom put me through. I was eventually freed from my tormentors, but there was a steep price to be paid before all was said and done.

Bethany posted the thread with the title 'QuikTrip mayhem triggers trauma', then stood in preparation for cleaning up the kitchen. She didn't expect a response to come back as quickly as it did though, so settled back onto her chair.

I can see how seeing someone getting abused would trigger you. How are you and your daughters doing today?

Bethany recognized the respondent as someone with whom she'd spoken at length on other occasions. Both women had opened up about their abusive spouses, finding comfort in shared experiences. It was one of the reasons Bethany returned to the chat room continually because speaking to those who'd been there and suffered in a similar way as she'd suffered was preferable to speaking with someone with only a book knowledge and zero experience; someone who could possibly sympathize but in no way empathize.

I'm so very proud of the women my daughters are becoming. They still struggle now and again, but they've always had an enviable resilience that I wish I had. Granted, their struggles were short-lived comparatively, but…well, they lost their dad in an accident, but they were so very young when that happened. There were tears all around, but we kept moving forward. Our lives really took a turn for the worse when I married their stepfather. For years, our foundation was really shaken. Bethany responded and *My Strength Is Me* replied again:

I get you. I've been there. Twice now, I've seen fit to fall for the stereotypical bad guy. Regretted it both times. But we survived, right? We're still standing? You are still standing, aren't you?

Still standing, yes, Bethany typed with a wry grin.

Then hold your head up, girl. You defeated the dragon.

He was definitely that.

"Mom, you home?" The call, in unison, told her that the twins had arrived back.

Thank you for the much-needed boost. Two of my daughters just got home, so I have to sign off. It always seems that my conversations here are so short and constantly interrupted. Sorry I don't have more time today.

With four daughters, I can certainly understand. Enjoy your family. We'll talk again later. Take care and stay safe.

You too. Bye for now.

"Mom, you here?" The girls called again.

"Did you see my car in the driveway?" Bethany returned, quickly shutting down Chrome and turning off

117

her laptop. She'd no sooner stood than her twins slammed into her, nearly toppling her onto her bottom. "Well, I'm happy to see you two too, now what do y'all want?"

"What? Can't we give our mom a hug?" Julia asked sweetly.

"When you ask me that in that impish tone of yours?"

"Can we go to a movie with Angela?"

"You mean you haven't blown through your allowance yet?"

"Well…"

"Ah…there it is. That's why the sugary sweetness. Y'all want money for the theater."

"Please?" Both implored, putting on their purest angelic grins.

"You know it's a school night, yeah?"

"The movie lets out at nine thirty. We'll be home and in bed by ten."

"Okay, who's paying. I'll transfer the money to them."

"It's my turn," Tanya piped up. "Julia paid last time."

"Okay, I'm going to go for a drive in a bit, so if I'm not home when you get back, make certain—"

"We lock the doors and get to bed by ten. We will, Mom."

"Have y'all eaten?"

"Yes, we ate at Angela's. Love you. We gotta run. Angela's waiting on us. We're going to hang out for a bit before going to the theater. That's okay, right?"

"Yes," Bethany barely had time to say before her twins were racing out the front door. She let out a huge sigh when her whirlwind twins departed. They always left her feeling as if she'd been picked up and spun about by a tornado. She was also grateful that she was exceptionally frugal as a rule, so that when the girls wanted something a little extra, she could give it to them without concern. She might have a large chunk of the insurance proceeds remaining, but she wasn't taking any chances where financial security was concerned. The week after Shane departed their lives, she returned to work. More as a defiance against Shane having prevented her working for a majority of their marriage, and partially because she never enjoyed remaining idle.

Of all the career paths she could have taken, she'd chosen to start work as a painter. Not an artist, but rather a house painter. She enjoyed the work, enjoyed the autonomy. The pay was good when there was work to be had. It took a while to build a reputation and a client base with references, but now she was one of the first to be called when someone needed work done.

She jotted a note on the pad next to her desk to add the girls' transfer to her spreadsheet tomorrow and then went to her room to collect her disposable booties and coveralls. She had her work clothes, but she never wore those when she went out on one of her drives because she never knew what type of 'work' she'd encounter. With disposable gear, blood spatters would never be an issue.

"I'll need to make a run to Home Depot," she muttered as she tugged on the coverings. "Almost out of these coveralls." She continued the one-sided conversation as she reached inside a small satchel and retrieved a painter's mask, a few pairs of nitrile gloves, some of her heavy-duty zip ties, and a roll of duct tape. "I may need to move these to the garage. Put them in the toolbox," she continued, as she did every time she went through this routine. "Less suspicious to find these in the garage than here in my closet." She constantly told herself to remove them from her closet, but she never ended up doing it. She shoved the items into her pockets, grabbed her keys, and headed out the front door.

She popped the trunk and went to check, and prep, her only other piece of equipment: her taser. The taser she kept beneath the spare tire in her trunk. The disposable work gear she could explain away to her children, but a taser would raise too many questions. She pulled it out and checked to ensure it was ready to go, then climbed into her Olds and headed out on her rounds.

It had taken a week for her to get up the courage to go out on one of her drives again. Despite her determination to rid the world of abusive people; despite her assurances to the police that she wouldn't stop until they were all gone, the last time had nearly been her undoing, had brutalized her soul more than she'd anticipated. Plus killing two people in a single night risked mistakes that she worked hard to avoid.

But seeing that man in the QuikTrip parking lot earlier in the day, terrorizing his partner, taking advantage of her diminutive size had her heart raging. All she could do was envision that woman being one of her daughters. It was as if someone was providing the impetus she needed to keep going until she couldn't go any further.

So, she found it fortuitous that her twins decided on a movie this evening. That meant she could go out sooner and get home sooner.

She got onto I-20, but less than ten minutes later, she got off the exit for Bill Kennedy Way and then pulled into the parking lot of the Kroger shopping

121

center. She sat for a minute and then snorted because when she left the house, she had a plan, but generally had no idea where she was going, nor who was going to be her next victim.

With a shake of her head, she pulled out her cellphone and opened the ColorNote app on her phone where she notated addresses from her previous drives, drives that didn't end in someone dying, but did portend death at some point down the road. If those individuals in those residences knew that she was on the prowl, seeking those who deserved retribution, they'd not ever commit a heinous act against their loved one, and certainly not in front of an open window for the whole neighborhood to witness. Some of the addresses came from her chatroom, people who revealed more than they should to complete strangers: names and addresses. Those who lived near her were placed at the top of her list. These were her preferred targets since she never had to guess whether the abuser deserved to die. Those she spotted in public or through a window could, after all, be having an off night, could simply be reacting poorly to bad news or a lost job. Killing those people would go against her agenda. Those abusers who were married to people in her chat room, on the other hand, more than deserved a visit from her.

She often thought that if there were enough police available to deal with people like this, she wouldn't even need to be out here tonight—or any other night? Then she'd recall her own efforts to seek assistance. Would the police dismiss them as they'd done when she called that one time, telling her to leave and get a restraining order? Would they do that with other victims of abuse? She certainly wasn't going to give them the opportunity to dismiss anyone else, not when she was ready, willing, and able to offer immediate release from their torment.

She Google-mapped the first address and then wended her way through the back streets, careful to avoid main avenues where businesses might have working security cameras. She wasn't overly concerned about her car being caught on camera, since traffic in business areas could be steady until around eleven p.m. or later, but she'd simply prefer not to get on the APD's radar at all.

Ten minutes later, she pulled along the curb opposite the first address on her list. The dark interior and the lack of a car in the driveway let her know that they weren't likely home. She pulled up the second address, punched it into Google maps, and then set off again.

This was always a possibility she had to contend with—that the person she was determined to slay wasn't home, or she'd find out that it wasn't doable at the house because the abuser lived with too many people. More times than not she had to abandon one chosen target in favor of another because circumstances worked against her on that night. That's just the way it went.

Five minutes after setting off, she pulled along another curb opposite her second target's house and was pleased to see the lights ablaze inside and the focus of her intended wrath strutting about the house like a rooster—wearing only underwear.

Don't waste time surveilling. The longer you sit here, the more likely you'll be discovered, her mind warned her, and she immediately popped open the glove compartment and withdrew her pad and pen to compose her thoughts on this subject so the APD could comprehend her motivations. She'd only started doing this recently as a way to explain why she'd started killing. Before, she simply eliminated those whom she felt deserved to die and went about her merry way. No fuss, no muss, no pattern, no specific modus operandi. Just show up, pull on her coveralls, pull out her taser, and other materials, electrify the perp, find something from their house to use as a weapon, and make quick work of sending them off to Hell.

Recently, something changed. Knowing the methods in which the abusers were attacking their victims created a deep-rooted desire to dispatch them in the same brutal fashions. As the death toll mounted, however, she began to feel hollow inside and decided it was because no one knew *why* these deaths were occurring; why these abusers deserved their deaths. Although it may be obvious for anyone who knew the victim's struggles. Still, she wanted the police to understand that she was doing the world a service, ridding the world of those who would stoop to hurting those smaller and weaker.

She finished with her note, folded it, and tucked it beneath the strap of her bra, then peered through each visible open-curtained room but didn't see anyone else moving about. Fortune would be working in her favor this evening she thought as she glanced at the note she'd written below the address in her phone: **Margo said he likes to use his fists**

"Well, so do I, you son-of-a-bitch." She picked up the taser from her passenger seat and stepped from the car. She did a quick glance up and down the street, then sprinted the short distance to the lawn. Being spotted by a passerby was always a concern, but everything she did to prepare was done so with furtiveness in mind.

Keeping to the shadows, she darted on tiptoes, ducking behind shrubs. The noise from a passing car caused her nerves to jump and her skin to tingle, almost painfully. She continued to breathe in and out through her nostrils, forcing her pulse to remain low, herself to remain calm and in control. It wasn't a far dash from her car to the backyard, but it seemed endless. It always seemed far longer than the return trip, after the deed was done.

Now, standing at the back door, she only hoped that the dullard inside came when she knocked; wasn't already passed out drunk. In her mind, they were all Shane, all drunk and abusive sods.

Her pulse went into overdrive as his heavy footsteps reached her hearing through the thin paneling of the aged door, it's paint cracking from the inattentiveness of the resident. Why that made her ire rise, she didn't know, but her breathing intensified at the thought, and by the time he opened the door, she was more than ready to fire that taser, and fire it she did. The probes embedded in his chest, his body convulsed violently, and he collapsed.

Bethany had long stopped gawking at the effects of the taser; had learned not to waste precious time getting down to business. Too long and discovery by a returning spouse or roommate was all but inevitable. Too long and a nosy neighbor, who may see something suspicious while peering from behind closed curtains, might contact the police. No, she came here for a purpose, and with purpose, she got down to business.

Normally, she'd remove the probes before anything else, but something inside her told her to keep it connected—for now. Perhaps it was his size, so reminiscent of Shane. Bullish frame that could easily barrel her over if he wanted. Her pulse racing, she placed the taser on the floor and withdrew the duct tape and two of the sixty-inch, heavy duty zip ties from her pocket.

She wanted to duct tape his mouth, to keep him calling out should the effects of the taser wear off, but that same concern had her using the zip ties first. She'd never be able to defend herself against his size if he recovered from the taser. With haste, she wrapped the ties around his ankles, then pushed at his bulky frame until he rolled onto his side. She wrestled with the arm that was stuck beneath his side. It took far longer than she'd have preferred, but she finally yanked it free of his weight and quickly secured the wrists before rolling him onto his back again. By the time she reached for the duct tape to ensure his mouth stayed shut, she was breathing hard. She picked up the taser, ready to set it off again, but the man lay unconscious. Her heart was thudding inside her chest as she sat looking at the man so similar in size and appearance to her dead husband.

Both were burly, with massive arms and beefy hands, and each could easily have been contenders for cruiserweight fighters if not for the massive beer guts they sported. That beer gut hadn't made Shane sluggish though, because even though he was on the heavier side, he could still strike like a cobra.

A moan escaped the man on the floor and a sudden fear gripped Bethany's heart. Was he strong enough to break the restraints? She always purchased the strongest ones she could find. Still, she decided it was best not to take any chances, so she shocked him again. The moans ceased instantly. With a deep breath of determination, she clenched her jaw and stood up. A haze of hatred welled from deep inside her and clouded her vision, fed her movements. She drew back her foot and with a grunt of effort, slammed it into his side. He didn't move. Without hesitation, she began kicking him all over his body—from his face down to his feet. She not only wanted to punish him as she'd seen him do his wife, but she also wanted to ensure that he'd be in too weakened a condition to break the zip ties if he were to regain consciousness.

A few broken ribs should see to that she thought to herself as she began focusing her attack on his side. After another minute of what she considered wasted effort, she ceased her assault.

I'm just not able to cause you much damage this way. Sickens me that you're so strong, yet you choose that strength to harm instead of protecting. I've been here too long now, she continued her inner monologue, *so I just need to decide the quickest method in which to dispatch your sorry ass hide to Hell.*

In reality only twenty-two minutes had passed from the moment she'd left her car, but she made it a point to finish her business within a twenty-minute window to ensure a successful escape. That meant she needed to decide how best to kill him, and fast.

The decision was ripped from her grasp when she heard the front door open.

"Jerome, you home?" Came the question, spoken loudly but with a timidity that ripped through Bethany's soul. It was obvious she was hoping he wouldn't be home. She knew that feeling all too well.

With rapid movements, honed from timing her assaults over the years, Bethany yanked the remaining zip tie from her pocket, knelt down on her target's chest, and deftly slipped the tie around his neck.

Suffocate and die, you bastard! Bethany thought to herself as she slipped the end of the zip through the latch and pulled, until she could pull no tighter. She never spoke aloud during her assaults in case someone survived. If they did, there would be no identifying sounds that could be provided to police.

She heard him gurgling, trying to breathe, but didn't wait around to ensure he'd die before his wife found him lying there. She pulled the note from her bra strap, tossed it on the floor next to his face, then slipped back out the way she'd come, darting just as clandestinely back to her car.

She slid inside, but before she could close the door, she heard the blood-curdling scream emanate from the house. She quietly shut her door, started the engine on her emerald-green Olds Cutlass, and accelerated away from the scene.

Chapter ten

"Officer, what have we got?" Hardwick asked without slowing his stride as he barreled toward the front of the house. The officer turned to catch up, handing over the evidence envelope to Wilson, who'd noticed it and slapped the officer's arm, signaling him to give it up.

"Um…black male, age thirty-five, found in the kitchen by the back door. He was bound and beaten. Then strangled by the same type of zip tie that was used to bind his hands and feet."

"Deceased, I'm presuming?"

"Um…the wife—"

"The wife was home?" Hardwick queried, stopping just inside the front door.

"Arrived home during the attack, as far as we can figure."

"So, the husband's still alive? He's not dead?" Wilson asked, unable to keep the hope from his tone.

The officer started shaking his head, "No, his wife came home, we estimate, near the end of the attack. At least it would seem that way since the victim was still—"

"Cut to the chase, officer!" Hardwick snapped.

"Sorry, um, since he was still breathing when she came in…well…she did attempt to cut the tie from around his neck, because, according to her he was still struggling to breathe when she found him, but the tie is one of those strong, thick ones, and she just couldn't make any headway getting it off him. By the time the paramedics arrived…well, unless they had a super sharp box cutter or a scalpel at the ready, they'd have been unable to save him anyway."

"That the note, Wilson?" Hardwick asked, noticing the plastic evidence bag for the first time. Wilson nodded, then moved next to Hardwick so they could both read it.

Those bigger and stronger should take care of those smaller and weaker. That's always what I taught my daughters— to take care of those smaller than themselves. They always did a fine job of it too, sometimes to their detriment. One of my daughters nearly drowned once upon a time when she determined to help a smaller child in a swimming pool. Bless her soul. I lost my cool that day, but she didn't. Tonight though, I kept my cool as I determined that this man, blessed with size and strength, needed to pay for using that to harm his wife. Small as a mouse she is and no match for that man. He chose to use his strength to brutalize and terrorize those smaller. Well, no more. Now he'll be dancing with the demons in Hell. Let's see how he does against those creatures.

~ Seeker of Justice

132

Hardwick shook his head in confusion. Not because the letter was shorter than the others and less florid, but also because it shot a hole in his theory that she took the time to write the letters *after* she'd finished her killing, giving her time to reflect and pen a well-thought-out composition. Wilson appeared to read his thoughts and vocalized them.

Wilson handed the bag back to the officer and then they started for the house, trying to find reason where there didn't appear any, "Perhaps she didn't have time to go out to write a note—"

"No, the fact that the note was folded and tossed on the ground by his body means that she arrived with it on her."

"And was interrupted, we presume, by the wife, because he was still breathing when the wife found him. Hadn't asphyxiated yet."

"Which is borne out by the fact that she didn't lay it out neatly somewhere as she's done before, meaning she was in a hurry to flee the scene, so, conclusion is she wrote the letter beforehand."

"All the letters?"

Hardwick stopped walking and nodded, "So, we can only conclude that she witnesses, or has firsthand knowledge of the assaults before planning any action against the assailant, and so is able to pen her thoughts about it before attacking."

"So, then these are premeditated. They aren't random, rash, or impulsive, but how does this help with our investigation, other than to give us a little more insight into the killer."

"She chooses her victims. Her choices aren't just happenstance. She somehow finds out about the abuse, decides that's how the person should die, then watches for an opportunity to strike."

"Okay, so we have more information related to her formula, but, again, how is this going to help us catch her? We can't track down every person who's had a police file opened for abuse and put a uniform on them. And, well we know, not all abuses get reported."

Hardwick breathed in deep and released it slowly, then started for the house again, "No, we can't, and no they don't, although I wish we could, and I wish they did. We do know more about who we're dealing with but that's all. All we can do is hope that the medical examiner find's something in her examinations that can help us find her."

As if speaking the words brought it about, a uniform approached, "Detectives, the captain has information about the cases and has requested y'all return to the precinct."

"Get back on the radio and inform him we're on our way," Hardwick called over his shoulder as he ran to his car. "Let's pray the information provides the break we've been looking for."

"Um…shouldn't we have at least looked at the body before bolting," Wilson inquired, cheekily, as he climbed into their vehicle.

Hardwick snorted, "We have the how and are fairly certain as to the why, it's more important we find the who, so, no, I don't need to see the body right now. The medical examiner will let us know if she finds anything of note, and the uniforms are already collecting any evidence they feel is pertinent."

Wilson could do more than nod at Hardwick's new take on cases. Whereas before he would meticulously go over every detail, rarely missing anything, now, he was more focused on catching the perpetrator as quickly as possible rather than going over crime scenes too intently. Wasn't even bothered over not viewing this last victim at all, which was odd in and of itself as he was always of the opinion that the answers in the crime scene would lead to the capture of the criminal…but no more. Yes, he still hoped that forensics would give much-needed clues, but it was no longer his primary focus. Wilson could only surmise that this new hard-driven Hardwick had to do with their previous serial killer case—Christian Price. That case had taken its toll on all of them but seemed to hit Hardwick hardest of all. In that case, Hardwick defied Price's dictates on trying to find him. "Focus on finding the victims," he intoned, but Hardwick was intent on doing both—finding the victims and hunting down Price. In the end, the victims suffered as a result—at least according to Price. Now, Hardwick was driven to catch the killer above all else, allowing others to find the evidence needed to bring their killer to justice.

"You think we should've taken the time to view the body?" Hardwick asked suddenly, as if reading Wilson's thoughts.

"I don't know. Perhaps. But I get where you're coming from too. After all, we aren't looking for clues as to the identity of the killer—as you stated—since we know this isn't the typical MO. We know the killer, after a fashion, and just need the forensic evidence or other leads that will help us find her. In short, we know the how and a general understanding of the why, now we just need the who. Viewing the body won't provide that information at this stage, so…yeah, I get where you're coming from. Best we get back to the precinct to see if the captain has anything of value to offer."

"My thoughts exactly," Hardwick muttered as he turned into the precinct's parking lot. They met up with Cortez and Harding en route to the captain's office.

"Anything new?" Cortez queried.

"Mode of death," Wilson stated. "I swear, if not for the notes she leaves at the scenes, we'd never know this was the work of a single person."

"I have something to offer," Harding grinned smugly, "but I'll wait for share time until after the captain gives us his findings."

"What are we—in kindergarten?" Cortez jabbed at his partner as they all made their way inside.

Harding shrugged, "Too much time hanging with my wife, the kindergarten teacher."

"Come in, come in." Captain Parsons called as he spotted his detectives weaving through the bullpen.

"He seems downright cheerful," Wilson muttered.

"Let's hope there's good reason," Hardwick replied, picking up his pace.

"Sit down, sit down," the captain said, waving to the chairs. He waited for his detectives to settle in before sitting himself. "Okay, a few things to go over, but first, what news from the latest crime scene?"

"We didn't—" Hardwick started, but Wilson interrupted.

"—get an opportunity to go over too much because we got the message that you wanted us back here just after arriving on scene. What we do know…rather what was relayed to us…is that the victim was zip tied with heavy duty ties and strangled with one also."

"We also know," Hardwick picked up, "that the victim was alive when he was found by his wife, which means that she likely arrived while the killer was still on the premises or recently departed the property. We've drawn this conclusion because the victim was still breathing when his wife found him."

"So, he's still alive?" Cortez interrupted.

Hardwick shook his head, "The wife, in her frantic state, couldn't cut off the heavy-duty zip tie with a standard pair of scissors, so he died before the paramedics could get to the scene."

"Shit," Harding snapped, shaking his head in frustration. "Just once I'd like some fucking good news, man!"

"Thought you'd sworn off swearing, *jefe*," Cortez jabbed, teasing.

"What my woman and baby girl can't hear won't hurt *me*," Harding supplied. "I have some information that may help, Captain, unless you've called us in to tell us there's a major break in the case because the medical examiner or forensics found something?" He concluded, hope in his tone.

"Nothing from forensics. No fibers, no hair, no fingerprints, no footprints, no nothing. It's as if this woman is a specter, however, the uniforms have taken the informational research that Hardwick suggested and have a list of names that they have started crosschecking as Hardwick suggested—with social media posts, etc. See if there isn't one of them that has a history of abuse by a mother and a significant other. The good news is that there aren't nearly as many as we feared there could be."

"Then my news fits right in," Harding smiled, smug. "I was talking to my wife last night and she suggested we add victim chat rooms to our search. Whereas victims may not openly discuss their past traumas in interviews or on social media, they may open up freely in chat rooms. It's possible too, in part, that this may be where our perp is getting her victim list from."

"Won't we need a search warrant for those sites?" Wilson asked.

"Not to just go on and look around we won't. If we find anything of note that we can take to the prosecutor, then…well, we'll cross that bridge if we come to it. Good work, Harding."

"Not me, Captain. I'll pass the thanks along to my highly intelligent wife though. Knowing I shared her thoughts just might earn me some brownie points."

139

"Kiss ass," Cortez mumbled at Harding.

"Only my wife's," Harding rejoined.

"Ooh, I'm jealous," Cortez snickered, but a stern glance from the captain stopped their shenanigans.

"Captain, can we get back to the forensics?" Hardwick asked, thoughtfully.

"No forensics, Hardwick. Didn't you hear the captain? We are dealing with *la espectro*."

"Yeah, I got that. What's bothering me—"

"—is the absolute certainty by the forensic examiner that there is zero crime scene contamination by our killer," Wilson finished.

"You do realize," Harding interjected, "you two finish each other's thoughts way too often."

"Brilliant minds think alike," Wilson returned.

"Okay, enough. What're you thinking, Hardwick? Surely not that we've got a ghost killer on our hands," the captain asked.

"That would be new," Harding quipped.

"How many crime scenes have we worked where the killer didn't leave something behind? Fingerprints, footprints, strand of hair, DNA of any sort? I can't think of a one. It's one of the benefits of criminal forensics. Helps us put away the bad guys."

"And gals…don't want to appear to be favoring one sex over the other, ya know. New climate and everything," Cortez joked.

Hardwick shot a disgruntled look at Cortez and then continued, "In this case, forensics continue to find nothing except that which can be ruled out. Have we heard back from the medical examiner? Anything on the bodies?"

"Ah…just the first one, which is why I called y'all in," the captain said, pulling out a file for their first known victim on the case. He opened the file and scanned the information quickly then summarized it before passing it over to Hardwick, "First victim—we'll call him the dog beater—though beaten soundly with a belt, suffered heart failure. There was evidence a taser was used to incapacitate, so we've established a potential pattern with our killer there. It's also likely, according to the medical examiner, that the taser was the cause of the heart failure. Sorry to say, there wasn't anything on the body…other than the obvious cause of death…that would lead us to identifying the killer."

"And I don't think there will be anything on the others either…so, the only common denominators with our victims, currently are: taser to incapacitate, differing causes of death, a letter left behind at the scene composed by a well-written individual indicating a level of intelligence, and zero forensic evidence that can point

141

us to our killer's identity," Hardwick ticked off, then sat back shaking his head. "Am I missing anything?"

No one interjected anything, each struggling to come up with that one small snippet that would help. After a moment, Hardwick leaned forward, "the lack of forensics could be a clue. The fact that the killer is leaving absolutely no traces at the scene could indicate that she is dressing in specific attire. Okay, gloves are a given. What other type of attire would cover an individual so completely as to eliminate footprints, DNA from hair or skin cells, etc. Think!"

"Spacesuit," Harding quipped, but no one laughed. "Sorry, but it's the only thing I could think of."

"Backtracking for a minute here," Cortez said, "has Georgia put regulation in place yet for tasers to be registered? Or requiring identification to purchase them?"

The captain shook his head, "Nothing's come down the pike about it, so I don't think we can rely on that, but I'll make a note to confirm. Okay, back to Hardwick's thought." The captain picked up a pen and quickly jotted a note and then refocused on his detectives.

"The lack of footprints could simply be the terrain; a lack of rain means lack of mud—," Cortez supplied.

"She could also be a lightweight, so not heavy enough to leave prints behind," Wilson continued, "especially if it's been dry lately. Might also account for her need to use a taser to take down her victims."

"The last crime scene had grass, so that wouldn't leave prints outside the home, and we know that she's too careful to step around and leave prints in the house...well, at least at the scene in which blood was spilt," Harding added.

"So, nix the footprints as a possible identifier, so far anyway," Hardwick muttered. "Hair net could be worn to prevent hair from falling out. Gloves for fingerprints...how else could she be getting away with leaving no trace behind?"

"Should we assume that she's hanging around after the kill to scrub the scene?" The captain offered.

Hardwick shook his head, "no, because the chaos of the scenes would negate that."

"Right," Wilson picked up, "the scene with the dishes smashed and the blood...there's no way she could have meticulously cleaned all traces of herself from that chaos."

"And this last scene, she was interrupted when the wife came in," Hardwick continued, "which means that even if she'd started scrubbing the scene, there's no way she could've completed it."

"So, we hope that when the forensics return for this third murder, it gives us something that the second murder scene may have missed in all the chaos?" Harding offered. "Being interrupted may mean being careless enough to leave behind forensics."

"It's all we've got to go on thus far, but captain could you also have uniforms do some additional research for me? I know they're currently doing a deep dive into cases ruled accidental or natural, but maybe one of them could look at clothing that covers a body completely? I don't know how they'd frame that for their search parameters, but—"

"I'll make a note and pass it along," the captain stated, jotting a second note on the pad next to him. He was about to dismiss his detectives when his phone rang, "hold on a sec," he said and picked up the receiver. He listened for a minute, muttered something unintelligible, and then replaced the handset.

"Y'all aren't gonna like this," he muttered through clenched teeth.

"Another victim?" Wilson asked softly.

"Two more."

All four detectives stood simultaneously and filed out of the captain's office, "the front desk sergeant will give you the addresses," he called, then picked up his stapler and threw it at the wall, cursing a blue streak.

There was no longer any doubt that they had a spree killer on their hands.

Chapter eleven

Harding and Cortez were the first to arrive at the scene of their crime and immediately knew it was committed by the killer of their current focus. If they'd had any doubt, the letter being carried by a uniformed officer left little doubt.

"First on scene?" Cortez asked as they approached an officer. The officer pointed inside. "Living room", he said briefly, "crime scene entrance is around the back."

The detectives nodded and then headed around to the back of the house and made their way indoors. The carnage that met their eyes was nothing short of shocking. Never in a million years could they have imagined their killer going from strangulation or beating to dismembering her victims. Grant it, it was just the head that had been lopped off, but that was enough. The amount of time and effort this must have taken was staggering.

As this was, apparently, the more heinous of the two current crime scenes, Dr. Monica Percival, lead medical examiner, was on site, and had arrived well ahead of the detectives. They allowed her to continue her work uninterrupted and, instead, went back outside, and made their way to the front of the house in search of the first officer on scene. They found her sitting at a small writing desk in the living room, jotting notes in a notepad.

"Officer?"

"Quinn, sir. Officer Orla Quinn," the uniformed officer stood quickly and stiffly, as if she were a grunt addressing a superior officer. Harding wanted to say, 'at ease, soldier' but refrained. "Fill us in," he said instead.

"A neighbor apparently heard the sound of a chainsaw roar to life and thought it was suspicious enough to contact the non-emergency number. Apparently, it wasn't like his neighbor to fire off a chainsaw at eight in the evening."

"Apparently, this was one time calling in suspicious activity proved useful," Cortez muttered, jotting notes in his own notepad. "If he'd called 911 it wouldn't likely have been met with any greater urgency. So, the call came in around eight p.m. and an officer was dispatched to check things out at—?"

"I arrived on scene at approximately eight forty-five p.m. and even though I didn't notice anything out of the ordinary, I decided it was best to do my due diligence. When no one answered the door, I proceeded to peer in a few windows..." the officer fell silent.

"You might want to sit down, Officer Quinn. You look a bit pale," Harding suggested. "Once you've composed your thoughts, continue. The sooner we

147

know what happened, the sooner you can start dwelling on cheesecake and bourbon."

The officer cocked her head and eyed Harding strangely, but his tactic to distract obviously worked as the color returned to her face. Nonetheless, she opted to sit to finish recounting events. "I came up on the kitchen window, which was around back, and when I peered in...well, I—"

"Saw a body minus its head," Cortez finished.

The officer cocked her head the other way, her brow raising, "Are all detectives so unaffected by—"

"Gore? Death?" Harding supplied. "No, we've just had more years to learn to process it in ways that help us maintain our focus. Have you had the opportunity to speak to the neighbor who called in the disturbance...about the chainsaw?"

She nodded.

"Did he see anything out of the ordinary? Anyone sneaking around the house? Anything at all?" Cortez questioned.

"No sir. Apparently, he's quite elderly. He genuinely thought it odd that the neighbor was starting up a chainsaw, midweek, after dark. He never thought to do more than just call the non-emergency number to complain about the noise, since it was 'loud enough to disturb my television show'."

"Did you interview any other neighbors? Did anyone else see or hear anything?"

"I knocked on the door to the other side, but no one was home there. I didn't think the noise from a chainsaw would carry to across the street, and there's nothing but woods behind. Want me to interview neighbors across the street nonetheless?"

"No, Officer Quinn, that's fine. If anyone over there heard or saw anything, they'd have likely come across to inform you as soon as they saw the flashing police lights," Cortez concluded, to which Harding interjected, 'yeah right.'

"What we would like you to do," Cortez continued, "is to go to any houses facing this one. See if they have a home security camera. Any kind. Including a Ring doorbell. Turn your findings into the precinct. Until then, we'll leave you to file your report. We'll be in the other room talking to the medical examiner, should anything else come to mind. Oh, was anyone else at home when you arrived?"

Officer Quinn shook her head, then pulled over her notepad and continued with her notes.

"Are we ever going to catch a break?" Harding groaned.

"Not if we don't start getting more witnesses, and reliable ones at that. Let's go see if the medical examiner has anything to tell us."

"I'll be happy just to get some usable forensic evidence."

They stopped just outside the kitchen doorway, "Dr. Percival, lovely to see you again," Cortez said amiably.

The medical examiner glanced up from her task and grinned, "Hello Detective Cortez. Detective Harding. Since you two are here, I can only assume that Hardwick and Wilson are at the other crime scene?" The two detectives nodded. "They'll be getting their information from my colleague then, Dr. Julian Micas."

"What can you tell us about our victim?" Cortez asked, pulling his notepad again.

"Well, he's a white male, no wedding band so perhaps single?" That information caught the attention of the detectives.

"Then who was he abusing to warrant getting his head chopped off?" Harding queried rhetorically.

"Possible he just wasn't wearing a wedding band. A lot of men and women don't wear wedding rings," the doctor offered. "Anyway, a cursory exam shows burns from a taser, so do you think this is your psycho *she* at work?"

"We saw an officer bagging a letter, so it's highly feasible. Maybe that's what we should dub her when we inevitably bring the press in on this: psycho she," Cortez quipped.

The medical examiner chuckled, then returned her attention to the body, "I can't call this the cause of death, but he was definitely decapitated by that chainsaw at some point." She nodded to the piece of equipment, blood dried on its blade, sitting neatly in the corner of the room. "Lack of blood spatter could indicate he was on death's door before being beheaded, or he could've been dead prior…although I'm not seeing any other wounds that could indicate cause of death. Doesn't mean there isn't any. You'll have to wait—"

"—for your report for any definitive findings. We know the drill."

"Good, then I'll leave it to the guys awaiting outside to haul him to my slab and I'll get to him as soon as possible."

"Doctor, it's clear at this point that we have a spree killer running amok," Harding stated matter-of-factly. "Is there no way you can prioritize the cases? If not as a personal favor to us, then by special request from our captain?"

"That a fancy way of saying you're going to sic the hounds on me to get your cases kicked to the top of the pile?"

"Nah, it's just a spree killer doesn't tend to stop until we stop 'em and the fastest way to do that is to find some forensic evidence…either from the scene of the crime or the body itself…that can help us stop 'em. You feel me?"

"To keep the bureaucrats from invading my space, I'll consider it doing y'all a personal favor. This makes body number—?"

"Four. At least recently attributable to this killer. The body with Hardwick and Wilson will be number five if it turns out to be one of hers. Although she purportedly killed four others earlier in her career before deciding to start leaving notes behind and killing as many as humanly possible as fast as possible," Cortez offered. "You already completed the autopsy on body number one, so we've got one more at the morgue, and three more headed that way tonight."

"Okay, I'll inform Dr. Micas, when we both get back to the morgue, that we're prioritizing bodies that come in under this MO."

"Not really an MO with this killer, doc, except that we're certain she's using a taser to incapacitate and leaving a note at the scene. That's the only way that we're connecting these kills. Still, we can't tell you how appreciative we are."

"Just catch her so I can get back to plodding along at my regular pace. Too many bodies as it is."

"Yeah, and never enough time. We definitely feel you," Harding lamented as a uniform approached them.

"Detectives, the wife just arrived home."

"*Madre de Dios.* Just keep her outside. We're on our way."

The detectives nodded a quick goodbye to the medical examiner and headed to the front porch where a black female sat clutching her midriff in a protective gesture while cradling a hand, bandaged in fresh gauge. The detectives glanced at each other and then moved to stand in front of the woman.

"Ma'am," Harding started but didn't get far before the female jumped up and started yelling in his face.

"What the fuck is going on here? I come home from the hospital and see all these cops around and they won't let me get in my own fucking house!"

"Why were you at the hospital?" Harding asked, taking a step back.

"What?" the obviously dazed and distraught woman asked, suddenly subdued, her brow knitted quizzically. "I just…uh…hurt…um…hurt my hand," she muttered, unconvincingly. "Yeah, needed stitches and stuff."

"The way those bandages are wrapped, you appear to have a lost a couple of appendages," Cortez

153

interjected. "Looks like it hurts too. Why don't you sit back down so you can stay comfortable while we talk," he continued sympathetically.

"What the fuck are 'pendages?'"

"Fingers," Harding explained, wriggling his fingers. "Looks as if you maybe lost a couple of your fingertips. Must have hurt something fierce."

The woman sat scrunching her face and turning her head in every direction but toward the detectives. It was obvious she wanted to discuss anything but the trauma she'd suffered. They couldn't prove anything, yet, but the fact that this woman lost her fingertips, and their victim lost his head wasn't a coincidence in their book. And as Hardwick was fond of saying, 'there is no such thing as coincidence, there are only facts', and the facts here were yelling that this woman's husband chopped off her fingers and their spree killer chopped off his head. Made sense to them now.

"Did your husband do that—," Cortez started but was interrupted.

"Nah…he ain't done nothing…he uh…he ain't done nothing. And if some nosy-assed neighbor done said he did, they be lying because—"

"Ma'am, no one said anything."

"Well then…he ain't done nothing," she concluded weakly.

154

Cortez glanced at Harding. It was obvious that she was lying and that she was scared shitless. In her head, if she talked to these detectives, then there would be hell to pay once they left. They could only imagine the lies she fed to the medical staff at the emergency room so that they'd patch her up without alerting authorities. What she didn't know was that her hell on earth had been killed earlier and wouldn't be torturing her any longer. But how to tell her without it coming off as if they were presenting her with good news, was the tricky part.

Cortez shrugged and took a step back indicating that Harding was to break the news to her. Harding shot Cortez an evil look, but then settled onto the bench beside the wife.

"I didn't get your name, you know?" He said softly.

"That's 'cause I didn't give it," she snapped, but the fire had gone out of her. Either because the pain in her hand was making it difficult to focus, or because the drugs the hospital had given for the pain were kicking in, making it difficult to focus. Either way, she appeared to be losing her ability to focus.

"Wanna tell me now?"

"Why you gotta know? I ain't done nothing…" her words were starting to slur, which confirmed she

155

was on pain killers, and they were beginning to take effect. Harding had to start talking fast.

"Just wanted to address you by your name, but it's okay if you don't want to tell me—"

"Marsha."

"Thank you, Marsha. I'll let you know this quickly so you can go get some rest, but I gotta know if there's somebody we can take you to…um…somewhere you can get some sleep. Is there somebody we can take you to, Marsha?"

"Why I gotta go somewheres else?"

"Because, Marsha, your husband…well, I hate to be the bearer of such tragic news, but…well, he was killed this evening and…well, we can't let you go inside right now…so…"

Marsha tilted sideways, falling against Harding's shoulder, and started wailing loudly. Harding wasn't an expert on female emotions, despite being married to one, but he did recognize that these tears were less about her husband's death and more a relief that her torment was over. It made him want to weep. Instead, he wrapped his arm around her until she cried herself to sleep. Then he carefully lowered her onto the bench and waved a uniform over.

"I don't care how long you have to sit here to ensure she doesn't roll off this bench, but you will sit here and keep her safe until she wakes up and you can escort her to a family member's home. If you want to enlist the help of one of your fellow officers to see if they can't locate a next of kin sooner than before she wakes, then you do so, but don't you leave her side. If you need permission from a superior officer to get it done, have them contact my captain at the precinct. Understood Officer?"

"Michaels, sir. Officer Daniel Michaels."

"I'm counting on you, Officer Michaels, to do right by her. She's been to hell and back and needs to know she's not alone right now. You feel me?"

"Yes, Detective."

"Good man."

Harding went to meet Cortez who had moved over to their car and was leaning against the hood.

"All good?"

"All good," Harding replied shortly.

"Let's get back to the precinct. If Hardwick and Wilson have made it back, we can compare notes with them while we wait on the officers on scene to compile their findings."

"I bet they didn't get a headless corpse and an hysterical woman with missing appendages."

157

Chapter twelve

Fifteen minutes from Harding and Cortez's crime scene, Hardwick and Wilson were faced with a brutal crime of their own.

"Doctor…I'm afraid your name escapes me. Have we worked a case together?"

"I've only been here a month, and, no, I've never worked a case with you detectives before," the man, harried from his day stated, barely glancing up from his task. "I'm Dr. Julian Micas."

"Okay, well, Dr. Micas," Hardwick continued, "I'm Detective Hardwick and this is my colleague, Detective Wilson. What have we got?"

"My fourth body today," the doctor said tersely. When the detectives didn't respond he stopped working, leaned back on his heels, and sighed heavily, "Sorry. Long day. Lots of death. Let's see…what can I tell you definitively as of now? She was stabbed approximately eight times, probably more."

"She?" Wilson asked, walking to the side of the victim to look more closely at the face. "Are you—"

"That's what the breasts would suggest," Dr. Micas quipped.

"Okay, gotcha," Wilson continued, clearing his throat. "So, the victim was stabbed at least eight times."

"That I can see after a quick inspection. It's likely the cause of death, but I won't know anything definitively until I've had the opportunity to exam the body back at the morgue."

"Tasered, by chance?" Hardwick asked.

"Now that you mention it." Dr. Micas leaned forward and pulled aside the shirt to expose the two burn marks on the chest area. "Yeah, right here."

"Okay doctor, we'll look for your report as soon as you can get it to us," Hardwick stated and then turned and strode from the house.

"First female victim," Wilson stated.

"Who admittedly looked more like a man, so either our killer didn't…officer, hold up," Hardwick called. "Was there a letter found at the scene?"

"Yes sir. It's on its way to the lab with the other evidence."

"There was forensic evidence?" Wilson asked, incredulous.

"Just the knife and the letter, which just happened to be pinning the note to her chest," the officer replied with a mild shudder.

Both Hardwick and Wilson sighed simultaneously. "Of course, the victim was stabbed,"

Wilson said with a shake of his head. "And you know of nothing else that was found?"

"No sir, just a knife and a letter."

"Okay, thank you," Hardwick said and then headed for his car. "Oh, officer. Have you had the chance to talk to the neighbors?"

"We're about to make those rounds now. Want us to ask anything specific?"

"I just want you to see if any of the houses, facing this one, has a security camera or door camera. Anything that might give us a clear view of our perpetrator."

"Will do." The officer shot a salute, then turned and headed down the drive.

"What do you think the chances of finding DNA evidence on the knife from our killer will be?"

"Nil to none," Hardwick replied curtly.

"Yeah, okay. Head back and compare notes with Harding and Cortez?"

"Yeah, the officers will make note of any interviews conducted of any witnesses, etc."

"Which there never seem to be," Wilson concluded crabbily. "When are we ever gonna catch a break on this one?"

"When our research hits on something,"
Hardwick replied, "or our killer royally screws up."

Chapter thirteen

Bethany was exhausted. She'd set off in search of justice just after seven and had found three of her victims. Not only had they been home, but the last two had been in the process of harming or terrorizing their significant others, which set Bethany to seeing red and all reason and caution fled from her mind. She didn't know why she recently felt a surge in the need to dispatch as many abusers to Hell as possible, but something in her mind was telling her that she needed to seek justice for as many as possible because her time to do so was drawing short. She had listened to those thoughts tonight even though it left her shattered.

She was still worried over the first victim of the night, the man she'd strangled with her last zip tie as a last resort when his wife returned home. That already had her ire up, knowing there could be a potential witness to who she was, or at least to her gender, but she pushed that worry down deeply, so that she could continue onto her next target.

She pulled alongside the curb of the next house and had to swallow hard against the bile that climbed up her esophagus. She couldn't believe what she witnessed; wasn't certain her eyes weren't deceiving her. But then the woman ran from the house, cradling her hand and screaming like a banshee, which caused Bethany to jerk as if slapped. She sat blinking for a minute more then looked down at the note related to what Marsha had said in the chatroom: **Punches and kicks**

She stared at the note, confusion knitting her brow. Was she at the right house? Had he used a knife on his significant other prior and she just not know it? She shook the daze from her brain, drawing in deep, calming breaths as the anger threatened to overwhelm her—as it always did. After another minute, she popped the glove box and pulled out her notepad and pen. She wrote out a short note and ripped it angrily from the tablet, then stuffed it—and the taser—into her pocket. Without wasting any more time, she climbed from the car and ran at a fast pace toward the back of the house.

She knocked loudly on the back door and then spied a chainsaw sitting on the ground beside the porch. Her nostrils flared and her lips formed a sneer as she brought her taser up and prepared for her assault. When the man answered, she fired, then waited for him to stop squirming, shocked him again, and then again— repeatedly releasing her anger through her actions until he stopped moving altogether. She removed the taser then quickly retrieved the chainsaw, uncaring that the repeated shocks had likely already stopped his heart. At first the clunky and cumbersome piece of equipment sputtered and didn't appear to want to start.

No worries, she thought to herself. *If this doesn't work, I'll just find a butcher knife and start hacking off body parts.* But just as that thought finalized, the chainsaw roared to life. Initially, she'd planned to saw off his hands or his penis, but as she stood, staring at his face, the vibration from the chainsaw beginning to numb her arms, she changed her mind and removed his head.

Without a shred of remorse, she turned off the saw, sat it in the corner, and pulled the note out and placed it on his now headless body, then turned and strolled out. All under her allotted twenty minutes.

Unfortunately, when she left, she was still on an adrenaline high, so she was more than ready to kill again and pulled another address from her notepad.

Her plans for this intended assault nearly didn't happen when she noticed that both victim and victimizer were not only in the house, but in the midst of a heated battle. She pulled over to the curb with a heavy sigh and felt her pulse beginning to slow. But as she watched the smaller man brandish a knife in the larger man's face, slashing and slicing at him, her brow knitted in confusion. Where was the woman she'd seen before? Had she jotted down the wrong address? She didn't recall ever seeing two men fighting.

She reviewed the note she'd written below the address: **likes to slap**. It said nothing about two men, nor about assaulting with a knife. *What was it about knife attacks tonight?* She thought, glancing from the window up at the night sky to see if there was a full moon. The overcast sky couldn't confirm that suspicion. She returned her attention to the melee taking place and shook her head in bewilderment.

She couldn't see the damage inflicted but knew that the knife strikes were landing because of the larger man's reaction. He was in pain, backing away and clutching at his arms. She couldn't hear the man's pleas, but she could see the agony on his face.

Bethany wanted to intervene, but there wasn't any way she could help as long as there was victim and perp in the same place for an extended time. She picked up her phone, deciding to simply call 911 to let the police handle this particular domestic squabble, and she'd just find a different target. She was set to dial when a noise drifted into her window. The slamming of a door.

She looked up in time to see the larger man running unsteadily down the street. A glance in the window saw the perp slide to the ground, as if exhausted from the efforts of attacking someone else.

Bethany put the car into drive and was ready to pull away, but a nagging doubt began nibbling at her brain: what if the smaller man was an intruder and, more worrisome, what if the woman—the victim of the earlier abuse she'd witnessed—was still in the house somewhere? After all, it would be just like an abusive spouse to leave a woman to fend for herself against an intruder, just to save his own skin.

Since the intruder hadn't left, that could mean that the female could very well be in danger. This thought spurred her into action, and she threw the car back into park. After all, she couldn't sit there and allow someone to come to harm.

Just call 911, her mind supplied. *This isn't in your purview. You're trying to stop abusers, not defend against home invasion.*

That had her questioning herself again and she began warring against her brain as to whether this was worthy of her time and efforts. She saw a movement in the window, which jarred her from her mental battle. The attacker was on the move.

"I can't allow him the freedom to hurt whoever is left in the house, or to leave the house and hurt someone else. I just can't."

She scrawled her pseudonym on a piece of paper, collected her gear and raced around to the back of the house. She deftly hurdled the chain link fence, and without pause, started pounding on the back door.

Time was of the essence, in her mind, because she didn't know just how long the victim would remain gone. Having a spouse nearly walk in, once, was enough for her. She wasn't wasting a single second from now on.

She hadn't anticipated the person turning on the back porch light and nearly lost her focus, but ducked to the side, out of view, just before the door swung open. Bethany moved quickly, firing the taser at her target. She saw the body drop onto the parquet flooring and quickly sent another shock to ensure he would remain down.

She stared down at the man now lying incapacitated on the floor, confusion again warring within her: why would he answer the door?

She closed her eyes for a second to compose herself, then shoved the question into far recesses of her brain, along with the doubts that threatened to surface again. As she headed to the kitchen, she rationalized that he likely answered the door instinctively, or perhaps he wasn't playing with a full deck of cards. Either way, it didn't matter. She wasn't going to allow him to hurt anyone further.

Entering the kitchen, she quickly spotted a set of high-end carbon fiber chef knives on the countertop and grabbed the sharpest, pointiest one, then returned to the body.

She knelt over her target's chest, ready to drive the first injurious blow, but was suddenly startled into dropping the knife when she spotted the two protruding mounds on his chest, small though they were, which said that this man was sporting breasts. She knelt back on her haunches, her gaze pinned to the size A knobs.

Her gaze traveled over the woman's attire: oversized flannel shirt and grubby jeans—mud clinging to the knees of the material as if she'd spent her day kneeling in mud. Bethany's glance then returned to the woman's head. The hair was cropped sloppily, as if someone had hacked at it with a butcher knife. Was this why she'd attacked the man in the kitchen? Had she requested he trim her hair only to have him callously chop it to smithereens? She hadn't seen any hair on the kitchen floor. She shook aside that confusion and then stared entranced at the woman's features. Devoid of makeup, she looked far more masculine than many men of her acquaintance. So confused by all that she was seeing, she broke one of her two cardinal rules: Never speak. Otherwise, a survivor might be able to identify her by her voice.

"Are you the woman that was being slapped about? The woman of this house? Or are you just a home invader who decided that it would be okay to slash away at the person trying to stop your thievery? Do I let you live knowing that you're capable of bodily harm?"

She reached for the knife she'd dropped next to the body. The woman moaned loudly, startling her. Adrenaline surged through her, and she recklessly snatched up the knife by the razor-sharp blade, causing her to break her second cardinal rule: never act recklessly. Otherwise, she could leave behind evidence by which police could identify her.

"I can't let you live," she whispered harshly, then raised the knife above her head. With a grunt of exertion, she rammed the blade into her side, then swiftly yanked it free. The woman's moans turned to groans of pain as Bethany brought the blade down, delivering repeated, devastating blows. It wasn't until Bethany realized that the woman had gone still and silent, that she stopped her assault.

With a glance at the knife protruding from the right breast, Bethany pulled the note from her bra strap, yanked the blade free, tossed the note on top of the bloodied chest, then rammed the knife in again to pin it in place.

She stood with a heavy sigh then wearily left the house. For the first time she paused long enough to peel off her coveralls, gloves, head gear, and mask, then stuffed them into a plastic bag, something she'd never had to do to date because prior to tonight, she'd never shed blood in such a way as to cause it to splatter all over herself. She'd left blood on the floor near her victims, but her assaults had never been so frenzied as to coat her own person in blood as tonight.

She couldn't see the bloody mess on her black disposable coveralls but knew she hadn't walked away unscathed and knew with absolute certainty that she couldn't get into her car with them on. There could never be a trace of her at a victim's home, nor could she ever carry a trace of them home with her.

She returned the trash bag to her trunk and shut it quietly. Confusion returned when she felt a stinging on her hand. She glanced down and noticed blood seeping from a small slice on her fingertip. Her eyes widened at the implications. She took a step toward the house, preparing to return to check the scene, but the sound of a police siren reached her ears, and she could see the flash of red from the emergency lights. Her instinct told her that the guy who'd fled the home earlier had flagged down a police vehicle and they would be on scene in less than a minute.

Quaking, she jumped into her Oldsmobile, turned on the ignition, and slowly backed down the street with her headlights off. Just as she rolled through an intersection and prepared to turn, she spotted the police vehicle round the bend, then turn into the driveway of the home she had just left. Never had she been so careless as she was tonight, placing her in serious danger of being apprehended, and it caused her heart to begin thudding loudly in her chest.

She moved the gear from reverse to drive and turned onto a side road before pulling against the curb again, putting it into park and then laying her head on the steering wheel.

"Your unthinking actions may cause your daughters to lose their momma. That can't happen! Never!" she berated herself sternly before her wails of anguish began.

She didn't know how long she sat, crying, but the sound of more sirens in the distance warned her that more police were on the way, and she needed to quit the area in all haste. Her head was pounding fiercely as she pulled up Google Maps and plotted the shortest route from her current location to her house, then turned her car on and headed out.

"First though, I need to find a place to dispose of that trash bag." Cutting her last kill a little too close to being caught was bad enough, cutting her finger and leaving blood at the scene was worse, but having her daughters find bloody coveralls in a bag in her truck, to her, would be beyond devastating. Her daughters were her everything and she would do anything to keep from losing them. If that meant ignoring the noise in her head and stopping playing at avenging angel, then that's what she would do. She hated that she didn't have the wherewithal to rid the world of every abusive person, but at least she'd rid the world of nine in the last three years, five of them in the last week alone. It wasn't something she felt she needed to hang her head about. Because of her, there were five more people who would sleep better than they probably had in ages. It was better than nothing.

For her though, her nights would now be filled with prayers that the blood from her finger hadn't found its way outside of her gloves; that her DNA didn't turn up in any police database.

Chapter fourteen

The captain had sent the four detectives home the following evening to "get some much-needed rest" because there wasn't anything to be done until the officers finished filing their reports and the forensic evidence was logged. Prior to last night, the only forensic evidence had come from zip ties and duct tape—pretty much useless. Last night, they'd had a chainsaw and a chef's knife added, along with the letters, which appeared to be written more in haste than the others. With more and more data being added to their arsenal, they hoped they'd soon have what they needed to stop this spree killer before any more bodies accumulated.

It was eight in the morning and all four detectives were sitting in the captain's office going over the three letters left at each of the crime scenes last night.

From CRIME SCENE #3

Those bigger and stronger should take care of those smaller and weaker. That's always what I taught my daughters— to take care of those smaller than themselves. They always did a fine job of it too, sometimes to their detriment. One of my daughters nearly drowned once upon a time when she determined to help a smaller child in a swimming pool. Bless her soul. I lost my cool that day, but she didn't. Tonight though, I kept my cool as I determined that this man, blessed with size and strength, needed to pay for using that to harm his wife. Small as a mouse she is and no match for that man. He chose to use his strength to brutalize and terrorize those smaller. Well, no more. Now he'll be dancing with the demons in Hell. Let's see how he does against those creatures.

~ Seeker of Justice

From CRIME SCENE #4

Rot in Hell you demonic bastard!

~ Seeker of Justice

From CRIME SCENE #5

~ *Seeker of Justice*

The notes were passed around, and around a second time, as each detective read and attempted to digest the messages the killer wanted to convey.

"I'm sure it hasn't escaped anyone's notice," Hardwick began, "that the letter left at the fourth crime scene is short, angry, and far more aggressive in tone than in any other? And the one from crime scene number five is devoid of any explanation whatsoever. What does that tell us?"

"Well, for the fourth victim, maybe she saw him lop off her fingers and it threw her off balance," Harding offered. "I'm clueless about number five."

"She still had the faculty to pen a note—short though it was—to leave at the scene," Hardwick interjected, "despite being so enraged at what she saw. Maybe that rage was still present when she drove to victim five's residence, and she simply couldn't put into words that anger, so just signed her name."

"Yet, as you just stated, she still managed to sign her 'name'," Wilson muttered and then continued thoughtfully. "She's possibly so angry and irrational that she can do no more than sign her name before heading in to methodically stab this woman umpteen times—"

"What point are you trying to make, Wilson?" the captain interjected.

"I don't know. It's just a sense I'm getting, a feeling that a switch has flipped in her brain."

"More like she's flipped," Harding snapped.

"It's possible," Hardwick added. "It's feasible that knowing victim five was a woman sent her off the deep end to where she acted impulsively and didn't have time to pen a note of explanation, yet remained enough in her right mind to remind us that she was indeed the assailant by leaving a note with her name at the scene. It's as if she's capable of rational thought in the midst of irrational actions—".

"That's a whole other level of psychotic," Cortez interjected.

"That could also explain why, at crime scene four, she lopped off his head when he'd only lopped off his wife's fingers. It was seriously over-the-top," Hardwick added.

"*Ay Dios Santo Maria*! You don't think the second crime scene where the dishes were broken and scattered across the entire floor, and the victim beaten with every single dish before having his throat sliced with a broken ceramic plate was over the top, dude?" Cortez asked, incredulously.

"Over the top, yes, but a more controlled over the top. The assailant had hit his wife over the head with a plate of dinner food, so our killer ensures that he's attacked in a similar manner. More excessive, yes, but the rage wasn't there, just a more frenzied indignation," Hardwick explained. "With the chainsaw incident, the rage begins when she witnesses the attack on the wife, that rage feeds itself to the point where tasing the husband and cutting off his fingers wasn't good enough for her. She tased him multiple times until his heart stopped beating—which was suggested, but hasn't yet been confirmed, by Dr. Percival—yet she was still seeing red to where the only act she could commit, that would satisfy her level of fury, was to chop off his head. I think she's losing control."

"Do you think that this loss of control may work in our favor?" Harding added, his tone hopeful. "That she may screw up and leave us something behind that may help us in identifying her?"

Hardwick drew in a breath thoughtfully and let it out slowly. "All we can do is wait for news on that front."

"Okay then," the captain nodded sharply, "we've analyzed the notes left at the scene and have added relevant information to her file. Here's the notes from the officers first on scene, the witness interview…" the captain stopped speaking and slapped the folder on his desk, "I am still having difficulty coming to terms with the fact that this woman appears to be a ninja. No one has yet to see her."

"At least no one that's willing to come forward," Wilson interjected.

"And no surprise here, there were no security cameras angled at any of the crime scenes. I've also been over the officers' notes, and I've concluded there's nothing here of note that would further the investigation. That leaves us with forensics…" he closed the officer reports and pulled over another folder, "…from the second crime scene in which the victim died from exsanguination due to a sliced carotid from a ceramic plate."

"Our controlled chaotic crime scene," Wilson added.

"Right. Anyone care to hazard a guess as to what the lab found?"

"Nothing?" "*Nada?*" Harding and Cortez said simultaneously.

The captain nodded. "Other than confirming that the blood on scene belonged to that of the victim and only the victim. If this pattern continues, I think the lab will come back on the last two victims tonight as blood belonging only to the victim also."

"Can we not borrow trouble please?" Harding groaned. "Nobody is so perfect that they don't eventually slip up. We've got to proceed with hope—even if it's the size of a peanut—that this killer will be no different than all the others that finally screwed up and were caught. If Wilson and Hardwick are right, that's a possibility, yeah?"

"Understood, Harding, and you're right. We shouldn't presume that this killer is infallible. Just because she's managed to escape from each crime scene, thus far, unscathed, and forensically immaculate doesn't mean she's flawless. She'll screw up, and when she does, we'll be there."

"Now that that's out of the way. Let's move onto the research that we've got underway." Hardwick sighed heavily. "Have any officers found anything that might move us closer to a resolution?"

"There, we have a bit more in the way of potential leads, but there's still a lot of footwork…I mean, computer work…to be done." The captain opened another folder, "Of the fifty-six hundred writers in the Atlanta area, within the age and race parameters, they've managed to eliminate three-hundred-twenty-seven. Then there is the search of domestic violence chat rooms…I hope you thanked your wife for that lead, Harding—"

"More than once, sir," Harding quipped with a wide grin.

"Well, we've found six-hundred-seventy-three threads in twenty-two chat rooms with potential leads that the officers are going through now with a fine-toothed comb, with more officers searching for any additional chat rooms that may have been overlooked to this point. And finally, we have officers still going through case files for the last few years looking for any deaths from chemical asphyxiation, or similar, listed as the cause of death to see if we can't pinpoint our killers first victim. Those potentials will then be cross-checked to see whether there was a daughter with a husband who was killed within the same time frame—"

"—as the mom," Wilson supplied.

"Correct. Nothing on that front yet, but I'm still hopeful that it's a good search to continue with, and likely will bear the ripest fruit. Since we've managed to go the rest of the evening and into this morning without any further callouts on victims with our MO, I'm going to assume our killer has gone quiet for the time being."

"More like…has anyone else noticed the times these deaths occurred?" Hardwick asked. "Sorry if I'm interrupting, Captain, but if we have any more deaths, they'll likely take place between seven p.m. and midnight. Check the times of death on all known kills to date, attributable to our spree killer—or the times the calls came in, since TOD may not be available yet. All occurred after many people were headed home from work and concluded after many working people were abed."

"How does this—" Wilson started but Hardwick interrupted.

"It doesn't help with our investigation, but we do know that we should have all day to work on research with the uniforms because if our ninja, or ghost, is going to kill again…ninja…" Hardwick muttered and then stopped. "Ninja," he muttered again and then stood and left the room.

"Okay, we've lost Hardwick to his thoughts, which we all know isn't a bad thing, and if he's right, our killer won't strike again until this evening, so get to work helping on the research. I'll let y'all determine in which area you want to help. Now get to it and let's catch this woman!"

Chapter fifteen

Bethany pulled into her driveway at a little after ten thirty in the evening, exhaustion and regret weighing her down and the persistent pounding in her head blurring her vision slightly. Added to her feeling of intense exhaustion was the fact that she didn't know what to do with the plastic bag in her trunk. Had she thought that far ahead, she may not have acted so impulsively this night, killing two of her victims in a way that would cause such a mess for her coveralls. Yes, they were disposable, but when covered in blood, she couldn't just toss them in the trash, and there wasn't a waterway near her.

She'd driven around for nearly an hour looking for any source of water, but there was nothing. If there had been, she could've simply put a few slits in the bag to allow it to fill with water, tied it off, and tossed it in. It would sink and the water would wash away any forensic evidence. Luck hadn't been on her side in this regard, and so the bag remained in her trunk.

Between that and the cut on her finger, she felt things slipping out of her control and that had her anxiety elevating rapidly. She laid her head on the steering wheel and drew in calming breaths until she felt certain she could walk into the house without collapsing beneath the weight of her fears and concerns.

She ensured that the car was locked up tight, then drug her weary body into the house and straight to her room. She slid the keys into her nightstand and was just about to undress and climb into bed when a soft knock sounded on her door, "What is it?" She asked, trying to keep her tone light.

"Can I come in?" Jessica whispered.

"Of course, sweetheart."

The door opened and Jessica strolled in, sitting on the edge of the bed, "How was your drive? Help any tonight?"

"This is one night I can honestly say it didn't do me much good. My head is still killing me. Usually, it helps to bring me a modicum of peace...anyway, I'm off work tomorrow, so I'll likely be journaling and writing most of the day. Maybe get on the computer and talk things out with someone. Didn't you say you had an exam tonight? How did that go?" Bethany asked, deftly changing the subject.

"I got a ninety-three on my Biology exam."

"That's amazing. Well done, you! What about Katie? Didn't she have a final exam too?"

"I did," Katie replied, moving into the room, and settling on the other side of her sister.

"And?"

"Ninety-four in my Advanced Statistics class."

"Brilliant, sweetheart. I'm so proud of y'all. You make we want to get on Facebook and brag it up every day."

"Oh wow, Mom, don't you dare," Jessica chastised lightly.

"So, what brings y'all in here at this hour of the night? Just saying goodnight to your exhausted momma?"

"Is that a hint that you want us to leave you alone?"

"I know we're mostly yelling at each other in passing these days and don't have much time to really talk, but unless it's super important tonight, yeah, I'd kind of like to get to bed. But hey, I'll grab a cup of high-octane coffee and pull myself together if y'all really need me."

The girls laughed.

"No need for such drastic measures, Mom," Katie giggled.

"We just wanted to check on you. Make sure you're doing okay," Jessica added.

"Not the best day today, admittedly, but I've been getting the help I need. In fact, I made a major impactful decision today and I think things will start looking up from here, but shouldn't I be checking on your welfare not vice versa? Helping y'all fill out forms or helping you study or something?"

The girls laughed aloud at that, "Mom, you may want to consider helping the twins with their schooling over ours," Katie replied. "But avoid offering help in certain classes. Math and science were never your strength."

Bethany cringed as she recalled trying to help Katie and Jessica with their high school chemistry classes. She bombed at it badly. "Yeah, not my fortes, that's for sure."

"Probably best you stick to writing. That's your strong suit. And if Julia and Tanya need any help with their English studies, have no doubt you'll be the first person they run to."

"But they know to avoid help from me on other subjects?"

"Yeah, we kind of warned them about your weaknesses—and strengths—on their first day of school," Jessica laughed.

"Oh, but of course y'all did," Bethany grinned. "Speaking of the twins—"

"They were home and in bed by ten fifteen," Jessica stated, ever the mature one.

"Glad to hear. So, am I good to go to sleep?"

"If you must," Katie tsked and then got up to give her mom a giant hug. "Love you, bunches."

"Love you, baby girl."

Jessica walked over and made it a group hug, "Love you, Mom."

"Love you too, baby girl."

"Hey Jess, don't you love me?" Katie whined, good naturedly.

"Only because I have to," Jessica teased.

"Okay, out you two, before this erupts into World War III." She reached out to shoo them away.

"What happened to your finger?" Jessica, ever the observant one, queried concernedly.

Bethany glanced at the cut, which had stopped bleeding, and tried to think of a plausible explanation. Her mind drew a blank.

Katie saw the perplexed look on her mom's face and glanced at her sister, "I'll go grab the hydrogen peroxide, antibiotic, and a band-aid. Don't need that getting infected, especially since you don't rightly know how it happened."

Bethany remained quiet, gnawing on her lower lip. Jessica sat down next to her and took her mom's hand in her own, "Is there anything you need to talk about, Mom? I know you always say you don't like

185

'dumping' on us girls, but you've got to know we're here if you need us. Right?"

Bethany nodded but couldn't find her voice at that moment. Seeing the cut again, drove home the fear that she'd made an irrevocable mistake tonight. She remained pensive and silent as Katie quickly tended her cut. When done, the girls leaned down and placed a kiss on each cheek, then quietly headed out.

"Night, Mom," Katie said softly. "Try to get some rest."

It wasn't lost on Bethany, as she stiffly stood and stripped off her clothing, that the stress and the weight bearing down on her shoulders hadn't lifted, as they usually do when she spent even a moment or two in the company of her children. The pounding in her head, which usually subsided also, hadn't abated. Normally, joy returned when chatting with them.

A person from her chat room suggested that the trauma they'd suffered, as a unit, created a specific dynamic in their mother-daughter relationship, one that could have gone in polar-opposite directions: complete breakdown or tighter knit. Bethany was grateful that she and her daughters had an exceptionally tight-knit relationship. One based on love and mutual respect.

Her continued elevated anxiety meant that her sleep through the night was restless, and she woke the next morning, earlier than usual, more fatigued than the night before. Still, she took advantage of the early morning hours deciding to make everyone a big breakfast, something she'd not had an opportunity to do since her two oldest started working and taking night classes at the local college. She'd hoped a familiar task would ease her mind, and it worked. She grinned when bleary-eyed individuals started shuffling into the kitchen after smelling the bacon.

"If you brush your teeth and get ready a mite bit early," she told the twins, "you can have some of this yummy food before heading to school."

Both muttered, "kk" before turning and shuffling for the bathroom.

"Do I smell bacon?" A bright-eyed and bushy-tailed Katie came bounding into the kitchen, followed by a less-enthusiastic Jessica.

"I understand you two don't have school today. I don't know what plans y'all have—"

"I'm headed to the library to study with Cindy," Katie piped up. "Headed out in about an hour. Then it's off to work later this afternoon."

"Same, just not studying with Cindy," Jessica yawned.

"Want me to drive y'all?"

"Nah, we're taking the bus."

187

"Okay, well, breakfast will be ready in about ten minutes if y'all want to go brush your teeth and get dressed."

"Thanks, Mom. This is nice. Haven't had a family breakfast in forever." Her ever-cheerful Katie bounded down the hall and Jessica shuffled after with a muted, "this is really nice of you, mom" that Bethany barely understood.

As she cracked open an egg, Bethany's gaze fell on the bandage that Katie had lovingly applied the night before and her thoughts drifted away again to that last crime scene. Bethany wracked her brain, convinced—as she could be—that her DNA wasn't on file anywhere, so unless she suddenly became a suspect and was compelled to give her DNA to sample against anything that she may have left at the scene of her last kill...she sighed heavily...there was still the matter of the bloodied clothing in her trunk. She had to dispose of that asap.

"Stop ruminating, Bethany," she scolded herself. "You really need to focus on something other than what's going to aggravate this persistent headache," she mumbled, as she finished up the eggs.

"What's that, mom?" Katie asked, gliding into the kitchen.

"Oh, just making some mental notes of things to do today. Want to start getting the plates ready?"

Soon after, all the girls came in and set to helping. A few minutes later, each grabbed a plate and settled on the couch in the living room to chat about a current video they'd found hysterically funny on TikTok. Bethany ate in silence, doing what she always did—absorbing their joy.

The laughter during that breakfast lifted Bethany out of her doldrums and it was then she determined to stop her spree killing before she made a more monumental mistake that would take her away from her family permanently.

Breakfast was over far sooner than they all liked, and within a few minutes of clearing away their dishes, all her daughters barreled out of the house headed to start their day. Bethany waited only a minute longer, then went to grab her car keys from her room. She stopped at the front door and scanned the street to ensure no one was about, walking their dog or just strolling along. The last thing she wanted, or needed, was a neighbor holding her up for a chat. The sooner she got rid of the items in her trunk, the sooner she'd breathe easier.

When she was satisfied that no one was about, she dashed down the front steps and straight to the trunk. She inserted the key as quickly as her trembling hands could move, then retrieved the plastic bag. She slammed the trunk harder than intended and winced, but dashed back inside, dumping the plastic bag on the floor of the computer room. She fired up her computer to make certain there wasn't a leaf-burning restriction in place, tapping her foot in impatience as she waited for the aging Dell desktop to power up.

Although she knew she could burn small bits of leaves and debris between the first of October through the end of April, there were always exceptions, and she didn't want someone who knew of that exception calling the cops on her. Nosy neighbors were something she detested.

She glanced at the backyard through the window, suddenly grateful that her and her daughters had planted trees as a natural barrier around it. A fast-growing willow hybrid that had shot up and filled out within three years. It had taken them most of the day to plant all sixty trees around the perimeter, but as with everything they did together, it proved more fun than work, except during their lunch break when Katie, playing with the shovel, had dropped it on her foot. That wasn't the least bit fun. Nor had it been entertaining when Shane stumbled out before work mocking them and their efforts. That had put a damper on their mood, until he left. But the barrier the trees now provided was well worth it all. It would prevent prying eyes seeing what she was burning if someone decided to peer over her fence.

The computer finally finished its power up. At least, she finally noticed it was up. She typed in the web address for the government agency related to backyard burning and was happy to see none were in effect for today. With an audible sigh, she picked up the plastic bag and made her way out back.

Bethany emptied the plastic bag of its contents into the in-ground fire pit and then went to grab the rake from the shed. Fortunately, the trees in the yard provided a large pile of dead, dry leaves which she probably should have raked up a month or more ago but decided it could wait. Never had she been happier about putting off yard work than she was at that moment.

She raked the pile of leaves over to the fire pit and covered the coveralls, then returned the rake to the shed and collected the gas can. Without a second thought, she emptied the entirety onto the pile of leaves. It was overkill, but she needed to ensure everything in that pit burned to ash. She collected a few twigs so that the fire wouldn't burn out too quickly, and added those strategically, tenting them carefully over and around the leaves, then stepped back, lit a match, and tossed it in. The leaves erupted with a whoosh and soon a large fire was roaring, causing Bethany to retreat from the heat.

"What ya doing, Mom?" Katie asked, coming out the back door. Bethany's face went ashen, and she stared at the pit begging it not to reveal its contents before turning to face her daughter.

"I just decided to do a bit of yard clean up before doing some writing. With spring right around the corner, there will be mowing to do soon. Besides, I should be asking you that. Thought you were headed to the library to study," Bethany replied lightly. "So…?"

"Oh…I just got mesmerized for a minute by the fire. Went a bit overboard on the gasoline, didn't ya?"

"Ha ha. So, what brings you back so soon?"

"I got halfway to the bus stop before I realized that I forgot my textbooks. Can't study the material if I don't have the material to study."

"Good point."

"Anyway, there's another bus running shortly, so I need to grab my stuff and head out. See you tonight unless you're off on another drive."

"Nope, I'm done with evening drives," Bethany revealed spontaneously and then realized how good she felt knowing she was truly done.

"Wow…big step. Proud of you, Mom. Talk later."

And like that, Katie was gone again, and Bethany's legs gave way. She didn't believe in what-ifs, but that didn't stop her mind going through the 'what-if'

Katie had returned five or ten minutes earlier. The fear gripping her belly had her falling onto her side, doubling in on herself as if someone had kicked her in her abdomen. The tears silently racked her body leaving her drained and exhausted.

The fire was dying down in the pit by the time she'd composed herself, sat up, and wiped away the tears. She stood on legs, still wobbly, and walked over to the pit, ready to grab the nearby poker and jab at it to relight it if needed, but a quick glance revealed that everything inside had burned to cinders. No evidence of her bloodied garb remained.

Zombie-like, she turned and made her way back inside and straight to her bedroom. Without undressing, she lay down and curled up into a fetal position and soon fell asleep.

Chapter sixteen

It was nearing the end of the workday at the precinct, but none of the detectives on the spree killing case were close to slowing down. It was as if they were determined to find the evidence to stop their killer before the sun rose the next day.

Hardwick was busily doing research on an idea that had struck him during their meeting with the captain earlier that morning, while Harding and Cortez were busy assisting uniforms with the search through chat rooms; and Wilson was helping to narrow down the number of writers that fit their profile. Two other officers were sitting nearby still whittling away at specific deaths done in a specific manner: caustic chemicals.

The captain stepped into the detective area at quarter to five. He saw heads bent with a steady focus on their tasks and decided not to ask them to call it a night. He'd let them make that call when they were ready, instead he called out "pizza on me". The detectives looked up and muttered simultaneous appreciation then went right back to it. The captain went back to his office and ordered dinner.

A few minutes later, Hardwick walked in and settled in the chair across from him, "thanks for the pizza, Captain."

"You're welcome. Got something?"

"Maybe so. I think we'd definitely have more success with this than trying to whittle away at the number of writers in the area. That may pan out eventually, if we want to confirm data, but with the number being unexpectedly high…well, now I'm less certain."

"Okay, I'm listening."

"Ghost and ninja. Those were two terms that were used to describe our killer because of the lack of forensic evidence at all the crime scenes."

"That still boggles my mind," the captain interjected.

"Me too. Anyway, that got me to thinking. What if our killer is wearing attire that covers her completely—head to toe. I'm talking something more elaborate than a hair net, or Halloween mask to hide identity—"

"Like a ninja outfit?"

"Like a ninja outfit."

"You think our killer is wearing a ninja outfit?"

"Not necessarily a ninja outfit, but something that would cover her completely like one, but still enable her to perform her task, so to speak, unhindered. So, I did two searches: costumes and jobs."

"Okay, and?"

195

"Well, I've garnered a list of possibles. As far as costumes: full-body spandex suits, Spiderman, ninja—obviously. Those three were the more promising. As for jobs requiring full-bodied attire, that gets more extensive: Painter coveralls, masonry, laboratory, fire and rescue. Then there are hazmat disposable suits, which I think are the most likely, which are worn by: hazmat teams, chemical labs, painters, medical professionals, and forensic investigators."

"Why most likely 'disposable suits'?"

"I don't know. Call it a gut feeling. But I don't think this woman is wearing attire to her kills, then strutting along home and washing it every night. Especially if she has children, as her memoir purports."

"Okay, so how does this help us?"

"There are three primary places in the area that sell Halloween costumes: Party City, Southeast Costume Company, and Norcostco Atlanta. Although, I am leaning less toward it being a costume. Still, with only three locations to buy something, and Halloween not far behind us, wouldn't hurt to see if they have any records on file for a female costume sold, fitting the bill.

"Personally, I think that would be a waste of time. Unless she changed her attire for these last five kills, she'd have had that costume for at least three years. Remember, she killed four additional people over a span of three years, that we know nothing about."

"Okay, so scratch the costumes. That leaves—"

"Your gut, which is best. I doubt she's using a work uniform—"

"Which leaves disposable coveralls. Unfortunately, those can be purchased at most Home Depot, Walmart, Lowes, Ace…anyplace that caters to those particular workers, or people just painting their homes. And since it isn't likely that she purchased the attire the day of each murder, could've, in fact, purchased disposable coveralls years ago, it would be pointless to view security footage of those places on, or around, times of the deaths. My gut tells me we wouldn't find anything."

"It's still a good theory and one I'm inclined to support, but at this juncture, it sounds like we just keep piling information on top of information. The question we have to ask ourselves is whether this is going to help us nail our suspect if we do finally get a suspect."

"If she is using disposable coveralls, as I suspect she must be, then we can use this to drive another nail in her coffin, strengthen the evidentiary case for the prosecution. Damn, thought I was onto something, but at this point in the investigation, it isn't going to assist in finding her. I don't doubt that when she's identified, we'll find evidence of the supplies she used, and that will help us put her away for life."

"Okay, since I'm not of the opinion that she has a buttload of disposable coveralls in a box in her closet; that she does need to replenish her stock of supplies every now and again, I'll allocate one officer to viewing security footage at those stores near our victim locations, a few days leading up to the kill dates. It one of the longest shots ever fired, but we may get lucky and hit something."

"If we don't, we'll just be ready to cross-check potential suspects with their jobs…in fact, I'll go ahead and add jobs to our search parameters. That might narrow down our list of suspects faster."

"You don't think that's just muddying the waters a bit? After all, she could be a teacher who is buying the coveralls for this specific purpose. Nothing to do with her job whatsoever."

"True, but the fact that she went for coveralls—if my theory is correct—shows a familiarity with them, and that to me says that she uses some form of the attire in her everyday work."

"So, we're in search of a professional person who wears coveralls by day, is an author by night, and a killer when the mood strikes."

"That's if I'm even in the right ballpark with my assumptions. For all I know, my guesswork is way off the mark and the person we're looking for is a truck driving maniac who reads a lot of detective novels."

"I sure as hell hope not. I will say this—your instincts have served this department well for many years. I've never doubted them before, and I don't plan on doubting them now. If you like the profile that you've come up with for this killer, then I'm behind you a hundred percent."

"Thanks, Captain."

"Okay, I'll pull a uniform and have them start requesting access to security footage. Good work, Hardwick."

Hardwick nodded. "I better get back out there and let the research team know which new parameters to add to the search. When will the pizza get here? I'm hungry."

The captain grinned and looked at his watch, "About another forty-five minutes."

"Okay, I'll let the others know. Thanks again."

Captain Parsons watched his lead detective leave his office and sighed heavily. While he supported his theories, he had his doubts as to whether Hardwick was casting his nets too wide.

To anyone listening it might sound as if things were getting narrowed down, but the variables were simply too great. Hardwick's idea of the type of work the killer may be engaged in which would account for their attire during the killings, for instance, seemed far too unlikely a correlation. After all, one didn't need to be a medical researcher to wear a hazmat suit.

So, when their research eventually narrowed down the list of potential suspects, he was more than a little amazed that Hardwick was right on the mark—as always.

Chapter seventeen

"Okay, it's been a week of steady work and I've got to admit I'm both shocked and relieved that our killer took another hiatus. At least there haven't been any murders fitting her MO for the last seven days." The captain opened the meeting with his four detectives feeling buoyed over the lack of additional homicides, and then Wilson had to open his mouth.

"I want to feel good about that, but she took a hell of long hiatus between her first four kills to her last five kills, the latter of which she did in two days. So, while I'm glad for the week's reprieve also, I definitely don't think we should let our guard down or get our hopes up too high."

"Thank you, Wilson," the captain muttered with a heavy sigh. "Quick update: I did the necessary research on taser licensing requirements, and as of this date, there are no requirements in place for owners to register their tasers, so we aren't going to be scouring any taser records in the hopes of locating our killer."

"Not that she'd have likely registered it if it were required," Harding jabbed.

"I know this may not be the most popular topic…" Wilson started.

"Great. What is it now, Mr. Doom and Gloom," Harding muttered.

"Lay off the kid," Cortez defended. "He just punches holes where they need to be punched. Keeps Hardwick on his toes and keeps us from spinning our wheels. Ain't that right, Wilson?"

"Do my best, but I'm not actually doing any punching at present."

"What's on your mind, Wilson?" the captain asked.

"I was just going to ask after the current forensics reports."

"Yeah, anything on the latest victims?" Cortez asked.

"Not yet. They've got a lot on their plate and will let us know when they have something for us."

"Fair enough," Wilson sighed heavily, then opened a file on his lap. "On the investigative side, the fact that we've been able to work unhindered for a solid week made things go a lot faster and I think that we've made a modicum of headway," Wilson started, "more so when we added the additional parameter that Hardwick suggested."

"Do you have a point to make?" Cortez interrupted.

"Sorry. Here's where we are. We started with over five thousand six hundred writers between thirty-five and forty-five years of age but had only eliminated

202

three hundred ninety-two before adding employment types. Believe it or not, that brought us down to just under two thousand potentials. Far less, far quicker, so thank you for that, Hardwick. I'm not a hundred percent certain that we're necessarily on the right road, but if this is the right way, then the added data helped…at least for now."

"Data never sounded so good," the captain extolled. "Who's next?"

Harding and Cortez looked at each other and then shrugged, "Um, our data is not as promising. We started with six hundred seventy-three threads on domestic abuse websites, and while the number of threads we located only increased by ninety-four, well, we aren't really narrowing it down much. I may have to ask for a refund on those thank yous I gave my wife."

"Why's that?" the captain queried, his good mood quickly fading.

Cortez picked up where Harding left off, flipping through his own notes, "well, the issue we're having is this: all there is on those chats is talk about abusive relationships and wanting to do away with the abusers. No one reveals their age much at all and those that have are outside our age parameters and no one discusses their type of employment, which means we can't get a feel for anyone who may wear the type of covering we're searching for. In essence, nearly ninety-five percent of those on the chat sites could be our killer, just based on their rants alone. There are some seriously angry folks on those sites, let me tell ya."

The captain nodded, "Okay, let's just keep uniforms on that, because there may be something that we find when we get a suspect that may add to the evidence that we can hand over to a prosecutor. If we can match up our suspect with a chat thread at some point. Hardwick, what about you? Got anything on deaths by caustic asphyxiation?"

"Well, eliminating work-related deaths, the uniforms and I have managed to go through cases going back a few years thus far and we've located fifty in which some type of chemical was listed as cause of death. It's a lot and we're not holding out hope because none were ruled as suspicious."

"All accidental?"

Hardwick nodded.

"Harding and Cortez, you jump on that with Hardwick. Wilson, you keep working with the uniforms on the writers."

"And hope that we're walking down the right road," Wilson muttered.

"Again, I know it's a longshot, but this killer isn't giving us many clues to work with, so we need to find our own based on—"

"Pure speculative investigative work?" Harding quipped.

"Yeah," Hardwick sighed heavily. "I know we're shooting at birds with a pellet gun—"

"Which are flying at Mach speed," Wilson retorted.

"Five miles high," Harding added.

"But if we fire fast enough, we're bound to hit something," Hardwick concluded.

"Let's just continue to hope that our killer doesn't strike again while we work to narrow our results to investigative levels."

Just then pizza arrived.

"Pizza again, Captain?" Cortez quipped.

"I gotta keep y'all fed if you're going to be worth anything. Let's eat and then call it a night, okay? Start fresh tomorrow?"

Everyone nodded consent and grabbed for the pizza before the deliveryman could set it down on the captain's desk.

Chapter eighteen

Another seven days passed without another murder from their spree killer. Other officers and detectives had their own crimes to contend with since Atlanta was known to have approximately fifteen violent crimes a day, with at least one murder every other day, but for now, four of the detectives from Zone 5 had been granted a reprieve, and they took advantage of every minute of that time, whittling away at the mountains of information obtained during their initial research. Mountains that were now more like an anteater's hill. For that, they were feeling quite smug.

"I'd like to begin, if that's okay," Hardwick waited for confirmation and for his fellow detectives to settle onto their chairs and then opened his file. "I have some decent news that might help spur things along. Harding, Cortez, and I…along with the five officers you seconded from other departments…thank you very much…have managed to go through every case file from the past five years that the ME ruled accidental with some form of chemical or caustic gas listed as cause of death."

"That far back?" the captain queried. "I thought she stated in her memoir that she did away with her mom—"

"We didn't want to take anything for granted as far as the timeline that this killer spoke of in her memoirs. The only thing that could throw a wrench into this is if the cause of death wasn't listed, was listed as something other, or not reported as accidental. Anyway," he continued, taking a deep breath only to have the captain interrupt.

"I was wondering if you were going to take a breath in there somewhere." He chuckled and then waved a hand to indicate Hardwick should continue.

"Sorry, anyway, we've come up with two-hundred-fifty cases; however, only eighty-five of those cases occurred closer to the time we think our killer's mother died—three years ago."

"This sounds very promising indeed," the captain complimented. "What about jobs within our parameters who also moonlight as writers—"

"Oh, you're going to like this one just as much." Wilson was grinning like a cat that ate the canary. He opened his file with a flourish and then read off the data, "Okay, it took a while since we had to cross reference our names with the IRS database to ensure that the employment information was accurate which meant having to wait for the proper documentation to be filed—"

"Wouldn't you need a subpoena for every name?" the captain asked.

"Since we weren't looking at financials, merely requesting job titles, we were surprisingly able to have the District Attorney's office obtain that information without too much fuss or hoop jumping. Where it got a bit convoluted was when we encountered ten or fifteen people with the same name and had a job that fell within our parameters but some of whom aren't writers. Or they could be but simply didn't declare a job or income from writing."

"But I thought everybody was a self-proclaimed writer nowadays," Harding scoffed.

Wilson pressed on, ignoring Harding's interruption, "And, since we weren't allowed access to personal information aside from name and job title without said subpoenas…well, we aren't able to eliminate some of the names based on age."

"How many are we looking at?" The captain asked cautiously.

"One-hundred-twenty-two possibles."

"Okay, how many match the eighty-five potentials which are closer to the kill date?"

"A whopping fifty-seven, but we don't want to limit our search to just those. We'll start there but want to expand to the entire one-hundred-twenty-two possibles if that initial search turns up nothing."

The captain nodded approvingly and asked his next question with cautious optimism. "Okay, what's the next step? Try to find those individuals in one of the chat rooms? Find a connection there?"

"Too many chatrooms, way more data than we can get through. Plus, we discovered that most people use pseudonyms for those sites, which means we'd need subpoenas for real names. I think we'd find ourselves chasing our tails on that one. Right now, while we've still got a lot of data to wade through, the numbers are getting more manageable," Hardwick said, running his fingers through his greying hair. "I think it would be best to start focusing on those deaths by chemical asphyxiation. See if maybe the files might give us the names of next of kin—"

"If there were a police report filed, maybe. It wouldn't be on an autopsy report," Harding interjected.

"So, we match up the autopsy reports to any police reports," Hardwick added. "See if we can't locate a next of kin."

"Since our killer is a female and was married, she wouldn't necessarily still have her mother's last name though."

"I know, and that can make it trickier, but here's the thing. If we find children with a first name that matches up with one of our writers who also has a job that falls within our parameters—"

"And is within the correct age group—" Cortez added enthusiastically.

"The last names wouldn't be an issue and we'd likely narrow our list of suspects even further?" Wilson concluded.

"That's my thinking."

"That would be like winning the lottery first time playing," Harding added. When everyone gave him an annoyed glance, he just shrugged. "I'm just saying it out loud. Hardwick set down a good starting place and while it looks as if his theories might be panning out—thank God—there's still an enormous possibility that this will end in at a dead end and we'll need to start all over again on square one."

"You're starting to sound like Wilson, *jefe*."

"Oh shit, you're right."

"If we have to start over, we start over. Until then, we keep moving forward with Hardwick's theory. Does anyone else have suggestions on how to reduce our number of potential suspects?"

The detectives shook their heads.

"Okay, then—"

"Captain, I do have to share a concern," Hardwick said softly, "and one I don't doubt has crossed others' minds also. The fact that out killer—"

"—has gone quiet," the captain concluded.

Hardwick nodded.

"Is it possible that perhaps she met with a fate that, perhaps, she wasn't expecting? Went up against someone who managed to get the jump on her before she stunned 'em?" Harding asked.

"Our killer became a victim?" The captain queried thoughtfully. "It's always possible, but nothing has come across my desk and until we know anything for certain, we have to continue investigating as if she is alive and planning to kill again. Have to do everything within our capability to find her before that happens. No matter our concerns about her inactivity currently. Agreed?"

"Understood, Captain."

"There's also another thing we need to consider," Wilson added. "She took a three-year hiatus between her first four kills and these last five kills—"

"Think she's gone to ground again?" the captain asked.

"It's a possibility, yeah. One we need to consider."

"Okay, if that's the case, then we need to hunker down and find her before her trail goes completely cold. Agreed?"

The detectives nodded.

"Good, then start cross-checking those names and find that killer. Whether she's dead or alive, it doesn't matter. What matters is that we end this."

Chapter nineteen

Bethany hadn't slept long because her dreams had quickly turned to nightmares, and she'd been jarred awake. She glanced at the clock and was surprised to see that only a couple hours had passed. She stumbled groggily from her bed and went straight to her computer. She needed to process her thoughts, and, for her, this was the best way to do that.

She turned on the Dell and the monitor, then went to make a cup of coffee while she waited for it to cycle on. She returned a few minutes later and pulled up a blank Word doc. Long ago, before Shane, she'd journaled frequently and would often revisit the words before beginning another day's entry. That was when she felt relatively safe that what she did on her computer was private. Those days were far behind her. She no longer saved her journal entries, merely started each afresh. No more re-reading to see how far she'd come in her life, how many of her tribulations she'd overcome, how many hurdles she'd successfully leapt. Now, it was merely a cathartic release that was deleted as soon as she finished emptying her soul.

I killed my mother and my husband because of the abuse suffered at their hands. My husband, especially, because of the threat he'd become to my children. The other two I did to help out two women I'd met in chat rooms, who'd revealed more than they should have done in such a public forum. But they were hurting and so I went to their aid.

213

Why did so many years pass until I started killing again? What triggered me so that I felt the need to seek vengeance against all those who would cause harm; knowing that it would be an ultimately insurmountable task? I've racked my brain trying to remember what caused me to seek out and kill another, so many years after I thought I was done. Was it that I had started writing down my thoughts in a type of memoir, a suggestion by someone in one of my chat rooms to unburden myself? Rid my mind of all that I'd suffered, once and for all? Had that stirred up emotions that I'd buried so deep for so long that they burst forth like an explosion upon an oil rig?

Is that why I would see red whenever I encountered the slightest assault being committed? That I became so blinded by rage that I was able to carry out those heinous assaults as if my soul had left my body to do the dirty work, uninhibited by moral conscience?

Is that why, when I returned to my senses, after the last three assaults, I determined that I'd gone too far? Allowed a hatred to seed so deep and root too long that I acted beyond thought and reason? Am I able now to move beyond that hate now that it has sprung forth so completely as to leave me feeling hollow inside? Not in a bad way. Empty of enmity. Empty of the drive to seek out injustice and act as the hand of deliverance for those being abused. That impulsiveness has somehow dissipated, much as a calm after a storm.

Can I move forward basking in the love of family and guarantee myself that I will never suffer another event that could

214

trigger me again into killing? I can only pray so, for the fear that
gripped me at that final crime scene was greater than any I felt in
many a year. I nearly died for my daughters several times at the
hands of Shane and would have done so gladly if it meant they
were safe from his abuse. After all, had he killed me, he would
have gone to prison for the remainder of his life and the girls would
have been free. But to have me ripped from their lives by my own
stupidity when they are doing all they can to move beyond their
trauma…am I no less capable of doing that? Moving beyond my
past to a brighter future? Am I truly strong enough?

For my daughters' sakes, I must find that strength that
I've fought against for too long, become the woman I must be and
pray that I've left nothing behind that will draw police to my door.

Bethany sat staring at that final sentence and had
to fight against a panic which threatened to grip her so
tight as to render her incapable of taking a breath. She
closed her eyes, forcing herself to revisit that last crime
scene, berating herself again for her carelessness that
caused her to cut herself and possibly leave her blood
behind. She clung to a tiny thread of hope: that there
was so much blood from the victim that the tiny bit left
behind by her, potentially, would get lost, would never
even be collected, and tested. And even if they did
discover the anomaly, her DNA was not in the system,
so no connection which could lead police to her door.

Nothing in life was one hundred percent certain,
but when she opened her eyes again, she felt she'd done

all she could to protect herself against arrest, short of running back into the last house and scrubbing all traces of blood away. For that, though, she'd have needed hours.

With a final glance at her written thoughts, she erased the Word document and shut down her computer. As she had when she was married to Shane, she never left anything on her computer which could be used against her.

Chapter twenty

Another week passed and the four detectives worked diligently, day in and day out, to sort through the data, trying desperately to lessen the number of people on their initial list of potential suspects.

The captain was looking forward to their weekly update, looked forward to hearing of a break in the case that would bring this nightmare spree to an end. What he heard instead made him shake his head and sigh heavily, "Are you certain?"

All four detectives sat dejected, lowered heads nodding.

"Not a single—"

"Not one," Wilson interrupted.

"I've got to admit, Hardwick, when you suggested cross-checking your list of names with those compiled by the others, of writers and jobs, I was certain that you'd get a hit...hell, I was certain you'd get several. Now, y'all are telling me that of the hundred plus caustic gas deaths, not a single obituary listed a next of kin with a name that matches up on that other list?"

"We double- and triple checked," Cortez confirmed.

"It's feasible that she changed her name," Wilson put forward. "Perhaps she knew that she would be a suspect because of her history and did what she could to break all ties. Maybe even requested that her name not be listed in the obituary."

"If that's the case, she's not only intelligent she's a downright genius who thinks of everything. Just like Christian Price," Harding sneered.

"I really don't want to hear that man's name in my office again, and I certainly don't want to be comparing cases to his that may, in any way, generate self-doubt. We are not responsible for the acts of that madman and are not responsible for the acts of this spree killer. What we are responsible for is finding the evidence needed to take her down. Am I clear?"

The detectives nodded.

"Good, then what's our next step? There's got to be more data that we can cross check against our current data."

"The chatroom—" Cortez started, but Harding interrupted.

"Those chatrooms don't use real names, remember? So that won't work, and as stated before, every single person on those chats could be a suspect because they are all being abused or are suffering PTSD from a prior abuse. Narrowing down our list of writers was hard, trying to narrow down this would be nightmarish. And we'd definitely need a subpoena to get the real names of those people."

"Okay, so how do we go about narrowing down our list even further? We have…how many possibles?"

Wilson opened his file and scanned his current data, "We're sitting on five-hundred-twenty-two writers and two-hundred-fifty deaths by exposure to caustic gas. Only eighty-five if we stick to those going back only three years."

The captain instinctively looked at Hardwick, hoping to see the wheels in his head spinning. He could see he was thinking but no ideas were spewing forth, "Um…okay, maybe I can speak with the district attorney. See about subpoenaing the names from the chat lists. Do you think that would be helpful?"

"You don't really think the district attorney is going to allow us to go on a fishing trip of that magnitude with only hunches to go on, do you?" Harding asked.

"Not really, but the worst she could say is no, right?"

"Yeah, after cussing you out for having the audacity to ask," Cortez huffed.

The captain grinned without humor, "Nothing can be gained without asking. Hardwick, you've been suspiciously quiet since we all sat down."

"You know he doesn't talk unless he has something to offer, Captain," Wilson interjected.

"Yes, I know. I was kind of hoping he would. Any of you, in fact. Anyone got additional suggestions? What I don't want to hear is that this case has stalled. What I don't want to hear is that we've run out of ideas. I want something, no matter how small or seemingly inconsequential. So—"

"We run down the names we've already accumulated," Hardwick said softly.

"A lot of manpower and time—"

"No more than we've spent already. What else have we got? Our alternative is to place this aside and start working on other cases; to let this become a cold case. All I'm saying is give us one more week and as many officers as we can muster. Let us chase down every single name. We're bound to eliminate a majority quickly."

"How so?"

"There were a lot of duplicate names from our search of the IRS database, duplicates because we couldn't access personal information, only job listings. We knock on doors. Some of those people could be dead, some not writers, some could be sixty-five or twenty—"

"I get where you're going. We could rule a lot of suspects out by simply doing a good old-fashioned canvas. Get off the computers and get out on the streets," the captain concluded.

"Exactly. Let's rule out those that can be ruled out. We find everyone on our combined lists and start eliminating names. Those that do meet some of our criteria can be examined further, asked a list of questions—"

"If we can narrow down the lists, then we may come away with a doable list of suspects that we can investigate and interview further. Viable suspects," Harding eagerly agreed.

"I feel as if we're about to run a hail Mary pass at the end of the last quarter with five seconds left on the clock," the captain muttered, "but I don't want to see this one go cold any more than any of y'all do, so I'm giving you the go ahead. In one week from today, I want results though. Otherwise, I'll have no choice but to close the book on this one, unless our killer makes a return visit and hands us another body. Understood?"

"We'll need a targeted list of questions to ask those people who meet our criteria, or at least part of the criteria. Something that will help with our eliminations, or help to identify suspects, without raising alarm bells in our killer—"

"If we're even lucky enough to hit that particular bullseye," Harding muttered.

"And it's important that we impress upon our uniforms that they are to stick with that list of questions. We don't need a rogue going off script and spooking our killer into doing something stupid," Hardwick emphasized sharply.

The captain nodded. No one knew better the damage a rogue cop had when they went off script, or in the case of the Christian Price case, disobeyed orders. "They'll follow your dictates to the letter, or there will be hell to pay. Get to it."

"I may have an idea," Harding started, as they stood to file from the captain's office.

"Email from the ME. Y'all get back in here," the captain called. The detectives quickly returned and sat down.

"Watch you got, Captain?" Harding asked. The captain was scanning the reports on the last victims. The scowl on his face was not eliciting any hope, and just when they thought he was going to say, 'no evidence found', a grin split his lips, "well, well."

"What?" Wilson prodded.

"Looks as if we may have just caught our first break," he announced, unable to hide the glee in his tone. "Our killer royally screwed up—finally!"

"Captain, I appreciate the enthusiasm, but would you mind telling us how?" Hardwick asked, tightly.

"Sorry, just reveling in the potential victory. Our killer, gentlemen, left us her DNA at the last crime scene. Lovely sampling of blood."

"You gotta be shittin' me," Harding laughed.

"I shit you not," the captain concluded. "I'll have it run through the DNA database. See if we get a hit. But if not, y'all keep working on narrowing down that list of suspects. If...I mean *when* she gets on our radar, I want to be able to compel a DNA sample. We'll have her then, and there'll be no escaping that particular rat trap.

"That's the best news I've heard all year." Cortez drew in a deep breath of relief, then let it out with a whoosh, follow by a loud guffaw, "I ain't been this relieved since Price was taken out."

"Okay, okay, there's still work to be done, so get to it. Harding, you said you had an idea, so get going and y'all get this lunatic off my streets."

Chapter twenty-one

A knock on the door startled Bethany. She glanced at her watch. One p.m. That meant it was likely a solicitor. She was tempted to ignore the knocking and go about her writing, especially when having her writing interrupted irritated her no end. She began clicking away on her keyboard again, determined to get the idea down that had popped into her head while she was making her coffee this morning, but the knock sounded again, more persistent.

Bethany drew in an exasperated breath and stood. Heading for the door, she was ready to commit murder. She peered from behind her curtain at the man standing there, clipboard in hand. He spotted her, smiled engagingly, and shouted, "I'm with the Bureau of Labor Statistics and we're—"

Bethany dropped the curtain and went to the door. She opened it, but then locked the screen door in a deliberate act to show that she didn't trust him. The man cocked an eyebrow but kept his smile in place.

"Just spit out your spiel as quickly as you can, since you interrupted my work."

"I do apologize for my intrusion, ma'am. What kind of work do you do?" he asked casually.

"I'm a writer."

The man lifted his clipboard and ticked off box one, "Is that your sole source of income?"

"Why do you need to know?" Bethany asked, her hackles still up at being interrupted.

"I apologize again for the intrusion. As I stated, I'm with the Bureau of Labor Statistics. Similar to the Census Bureau, we're tasked with compiling data on the types of work performed by—"

"Got it. No, it's not my primary source of income," Bethany stated.

"What—"

"I'm a house painter," Bethany answered, anticipating the question.

"And your spouse or significant other?"

"I'm not married."

"Divorced, widowed, single?"

"Widowed."

"I'm very sorry for your loss."

"I'm not," Bethany muttered, but it didn't go unheard.

"I'm sincerely sorry. We should grieve those we've lost, not celebrate. Unless he was abusive like my sister's husband was. We threw a party after his

225

death—" the census taker stated, his tone genuine, but Bethany cut him off.

"Is that all?"

The census taker cleared his throat and muttered an apology beneath his breath, then sniffed and regained his professional demeanor, "Almost, and I do appreciate your patience. Are there any other working adults in the home?"

"No."

"Okay, final question. Can you tell me your name—first and last, as well as your age, please?"

"Bethany Barnstead. Thirty-nine."

"Okay, I appreciate your time, and I do hope the rest of your day is productive."

Bethany closed the door and determined to put up a 'no solicitations' sign as soon as she finished typing out her idea.

The plain-clothes officer walked back to his unmarked vehicle, climbed inside, and immediately radioed the front desk sergeant. "This is Officer Chavez, tell the detectives that I found one that ticked all the boxes."

Officer Chavez, I'm going to make a leap and say this is your first hit today, but you've got at least another five hours of names to chase down. So, when you've completed your list for today, you'll bring in your completed forms and can dance a jig all the way down the corridor to pass your extraordinary findings along. Until that time, your fervor isn't physically getting that form here to tack up on the board, which does the detectives zero good.

"Understood, Sergeant."

Good, then keep at it and we'll see you back here at the end of the day.

The past four days at the precinct had been a flurry of activity as radio calls came in eliminating names from their list, or officers returned, and they were able to pin a completed 'potential suspect' form on the board.

While the list of names dwindled dramatically with each passing day, the number of viable potential leads remained anemic. After four days, only four names and addresses were pinned on the board. Seeing so few potentials should have made the detectives happy. After all, this should signal to them that their killer was— potentially—one of those four people and researching only four names to find links and run background checks on was far simpler than the hundreds of names they'd started with.

"I can't believe this might actually produce results—" Cortez started, but Hardwick interjected.

"It isn't a matter of whether it'll produce results, it's whether those results lead to the conviction of our killer."

"The fewer names we have to take to a judge to compel a DNA sample, the better, in my opinion," Cortez retorted.

"Unless those DNA samples come back negative on those few samples…"

"Then we'd have to start again at square one with a new set of parameters," Harding concluded.

"And the likelihood of the captain calling off the search at that point, especially since our spree killer has apparently decided on an extended vacation, is highly likely. That means the case would go cold unless she cut her hiatus short and started killing again," Hardwick added.

"Yeah, but these are the most results we've seen since the onset of this case," Wilson added, "so I'm hopeful that this is going to bear fruit."

The captain had given them an additional seven days and they'd used four of those already. To keep from wasting valuable time, an officer was assigned the task of running down every shred of information related to those on the board: social media, family history…anything and everything, no matter how inconsequential, that was public knowledge and wouldn't require a warrant to obtain. That could be obtained later if they obtained substantial circumstantial evidence to take to a judge.

At the same time, Captain Parsons spent time drafting a request for a subpoena to access chatroom databases, which he decided he'd submit at the end of day. It may not help, but it would be derelict of duty, in his opinion, if he overlooked even one thing that could lead to the conviction of a spree killer. He hoped that by simply requesting the name associated with a username and nothing further—much as they'd done with the IRS information—the district attorney wouldn't just laugh in his face. It was a long shot, but this entire case appeared to be a string of long shots.

Thirty minutes after his call in to the desk sergeant, Officer Chavez walked into the precinct and straight over to Hardwick, "Detective, I know we're supposed to complete our list of names before bringing in any findings, but my instinct on this one is too strong." He passed over his paper, which had all the boxes checked marked, along with the suspect's name and address.

"We've had four other suspects that ticked all, or most, of the requisites. What made this one stand out to you?" Hardwick asked.

"Aside from ticking all the boxes, she's widowed, and when I told her I was sorry for her loss, she literally snapped 'I'm not'. Her entire behavior had my radar on high alert. I know instinct isn't—"

"Instinct is exceptionally important in this line of work, officer, so don't doubt it," Hardwick interrupted. "Harding, Wilson, Cortez, can y'all come here for a minute?"

The other three detectives stopped their work and walked over, each nodding to the officer standing next to Hardwick.

"What's up?" Cortez asked.

"Officer—" Hardwick paused.

"Chavez, sir."

"Officer Chavez, start at the beginning. Let us know precisely what was said and your impressions. Don't leave anything out, no matter how inconsequential you think it might be."

"If what Officer Chavez has to say is so mind-blowing, shouldn't the captain be in on this conversation also?" Harding interjected. "Keep us having to repeat everything anyway. He'll get it straight from the horse's mouth, as it were."

"Wilson, would you mind getting the captain?" Hardwick asked.

"This must be some powerful shit you need to convey, *jefe*," Cortez teased.

"That's something we're all here to assess," Hardwick interrupted.

"What are we assessing?" the captain asked as he settled onto a nearby chair. The detectives pulled over chairs also, leaving Officer Chavez standing awkwardly in front of them, as if he were about to deliver a speech. He was immensely grateful when Hardwick said, "pull up a chair, Chavez."

Chavez settled onto a nearby chair. When Hardwick waved at him, giving him the floor, he began by explaining how he followed the list of questioning as instructed, "but when I asked her about her husband, she mentioned he was dead. I expressed my sympathy, saying that I was sorry for her loss, and she said, 'I'm not', as in not sorry, but the tone was harsh. She spat those words out as if getting rid of something distasteful. I know we're not supposed to go off script, but I said that the passing of a spouse should be sad, unless they were abusive as in the case of my sister's husband…I think I said sister…not that it matters since I don't have any siblings. Anyway, her face took on this weird look, almost sinister, and she shut me down after that. Discussing an abusive spouse wasn't something she wanted to do—"

"I don't find that odd, Officer Chavez," the captain stated. "I've known a few individuals in my lifetime who didn't feel comfortable speaking of their

231

abusive relationships, so for her to shut you down—a complete stranger—"

"Yes sir, I get that sir. It wasn't that she shut me down, sir. It was the expression on her face that set me on my toes. When I was asking general questions about her, she was terse at my interrupting her work, but cordial enough. It wasn't until I brought up her spouse, that her entire demeanor changed, including her facial expressions. You know those universal expressions that most people are unable to hide or control when they're speaking about something unpleasant? Well, she exhibited nearly all of them, from anger to disgust. Anyway, she's also a house painter, a writer, and she's thirty-nine years of age. All of which are in our target grid, yeah?"

"Okay, Officer Chavez, thank you for your insights," the captain said, "do you have more names to chase down today?"

"Yes, sir."

"Okay, you continue with your work. Thank you for bringing this to our attention."

"Yes, sir." Office Chavez departed leaving the detectives and the captain sitting silent, thoughtful.

"Chalk it up to enthusiasm?" Harding asked finally.

"He genuinely got a sense for this one. Do we really want to ignore that?" Wilson asked.

"We don't ignore it, no," the captain added. "We add her form to the board and investigate her along with our other suspects. While I respect the officer's enthusiasm, it isn't definitive proof of guilt."

"Agreed," Cortez affirmed.

"Let's just put her name at the top of the board as one of those to interview first, when we get to that point. Since we all know that instinct isn't something we should overlook completely, even in a rookie officer. Fair enough?" Hardwick added.

The detectives nodded and everyone stood to resume their tasks. What they didn't know was that the visit to Bethany's house triggered her emotions, deeply buried, sending her into a murderous rage.

Chapter twenty-two

Bethany attempted to return to her writing. She'd been in the process of killing off one of her characters when the solicitor interrupted her thoughts but was now struggling to determine how to move forward. Her thoughts were a jumble, and her emotions were in turmoil, which meant that writing wasn't possible. She paced for a while, trying to deep-breathe her way back into a calm mental state, but even that was proving a trying task. She glanced at her watch. It was only one thirty-five p.m. There was still two and a half hours before the twins arrived home from school.

Her thoughts went to the list of potential targets she'd deleted from her phone and her nostrils flared. If she went for one of her drives…she stopped the thought in its tracks. She was more than ill-prepared. She'd tossed all her disposable coveralls, which meant that she'd have to wear her work gear. That was too great a risk. She could run by the Home Depot and snare a set, but did she really want to take the time to do that, then drive around in broad daylight on the prowl of a deserving abuser? In her experience, many were at work during the day, or, like her now-dead husband, worked nights and slept the day away.

Instead of calming her, the thought of not being prepared to take someone out, had her temper elevating, and she was having a difficult time suppressing the urge to kill.

Her glance moved to the backyard where some downed branches, from the winter storms, still lay awaiting her attention. With jerky movements, she stormed to the back, pulled on her yard shoes, and grabbed her axe from the shed. With little hesitation, or regard for flying debris, she started whacking furiously at the pile, envisioning Shane's face with every strike.

It wasn't until a shard flew up and jabbed her arm that she was startled back to the present, jerked out of her thoughts. She looked at the axe in her hand and momentarily was unable to recall how it got there. She then looked at the mess of logs and sticks, scattered from the repeated battering, and let loose a long sigh. She turned and replaced the axe in the shed, went inside, slipping her shoes off at the door, then settled onto the couch in the living room. As was her habit of late, she curled up into a ball and started crying, incapable of controlling the overwhelming emotions that struck her when she acted irrationally, a level that bordered on insanity.

The airbrakes from the school bus pulled her from her dejected state and she sat up, swiped her eyes, and went to the kitchen to prepare a snack for herself and the twins. Her heart still ached, and her head still hurt, but she was back in control for the time being, for which she felt eternally grateful. Without a doubt, today's episode left her feeling agitated, so the sooner she could get on her computer to discuss her feelings with someone in her chat group, the better she'd feel.

"In the kitchen," she shouted when she heard the front door open and the laughter from her girls reach her hearing.

"No work today?" Julia asked, grabbing at a piece of fruit on the plate.

"Disappointed?" Bethany joked. "Worried I may pull my computer into the living room and make you girls work on homework before starting your video games?" Tanya's face took on a sheepish grin and Bethany laughed, "who knows her baby girls?"

"Can't we play one round of—"

"Why is it always a surprise to you two that I expect you to do your homework first? We've only been doing this since—"

"We were born, we know," Julia moaned.

Bethany grinned, "Go set your stuff down and come have your snack. We'll meet in the living room in a few minutes. The sooner we get started, the sooner we finish."

That was rarely the case, as the girls' homework got more complex with each passing year. Bethany was grateful for those days when Jessica or Katie was home so they could assist, since they were closer to the newer subjects than she was. Still, she did her best, researching information when needed.

"Aren't Jessica or Katie here?" Julia asked, as if reading her thoughts. They knew they were likely to get their stuff done quicker with their older sisters' help than with hers.

"I haven't heard hide nor hair from either of them since they left this morning. Speaking of which—" she pulled out her cell phone and typed a quick 'checking in' text to her daughters. Within a few minutes, both responded, 'still alive'. That brought another smile to her lips.

This system of security had started with the safe word 'dolphin' when Jessica and Katie were small. It was a word they were to ask of anyone who tried to pick them up from school, or another place, under the guise of 'your mom sent me'. If that ever occurred, they were to simply ask, 'what's the password?'. If that person couldn't supply it, then Jessica and Katie would know that their mom hadn't sent them.

As the years passed and cell phones became a part of their lives, the girls suggested creating a safe response, in addition to a password, so that she would know if their phones had been stolen or they were in danger. If the response to her query came back as anything other than the safe response, Bethany would know something was wrong.

It was, surprisingly, the twins who'd suggested using 'still alive' as the safe response, because a stranger could force them to say 'I'm okay' to any inquiry.

"Apparently, your sisters are safe and sound," she told the twins, "but as they are not here, it looks as if you're stuck doing homework with me tonight. If you need help, just let me know. I do have something that I'd like to tend to, so I'll stay out of your hair unless you need me. I'll just grab my laptop and meet y'all in the living room."

"Really? You mean you actually pulled that thing out of its box finally?"

"Just a few days ago," Bethany laughed. "Still haven't used it much though. Prefer sitting at my desk and using my desktop."

"Obviously," the girls laughed, rolling their eyes.

"I'll be right back."

The girls had settled on the couch and had their own books and laptop opened. Bethany smiled and settled onto her recliner, then opened Chrome and headed straight for her chat room. Although she was feeling somewhat better, these near blackouts, or a need to sleep, when she was seeing red were beginning to grow concerning to her as they were getting more frequent. She doubted that anyone in her chats would be able to help with that, but they always managed to provide her with some words of wisdom and comfort that brought her back around to feeling grounded.

She started a thread with the heading 'what's wrong with me?' and then phrased her concerns as succinctly as possible.

The years of abuse I suffered…I was hoping to have moved beyond the impacts by now. After 3+ years, I should be able to put the past behind me and move on. I learned techniques that enable me to function and focus, but there are times when I get so angry that…well, I can't say that I lose ability to focus or function because I do both just fine, but oftentimes, I feel as if I'm doing so as an observer. No, that's not right either. There are times when I feel as if I've become so angry that I detach from what my body is doing, but only some of those times can I experience what I'm doing. Other times, like today, I was unaware of my actions, like I'd blacked out. Soon after, I was so mentally and physically exhausted that I immediately lay down and fell asleep.

It happened because I got disrupted while working and the questions asked by the person somehow triggered me to where I was enraged. When I 'came to' as it were, I was standing outside chopping wood. Not even chopping, more like annihilating. I wasn't aware of my actions at all until a sliver of wood flew up and jabbed my arm. It took a long time for me to find my way back to a calm state of being, but I'm coherent again now. Peaceful even. What's wrong with me? Any thoughts? Suggestions on how to get past a rage so intense that it's like I'm sleepwalking through that state?

"Mom, got a second to help me with a math problem?" Julia asked. Bethany heard the reticence in her tone because she knew that math was not her mom's strong suit, but it wasn't hers either. Julia thought about asking Katie for help, but Katie was working on a literary analysis for her English Lit class, and when Katie was focused on her writing, you didn't disrupt her train of thought—much as with their mom.

Bethany glanced down at the thread she'd written, but there weren't any responses yet, so she sat the laptop aside and went to sit next to Julia. She'd hear a chime if anyone responded.

"What are you working on?"

"Trigonometric functions. This is the problem: If $\cos\sigma=-1$, what is the value of $\sin\sigma$?"

Just then the front door opened, and Jessica walked in. The twins put their laptops down and raced over for a quick hug, "Need help with homework, I take it?" she laughed.

"Oh, you couldn't have timed that better if you tried," Bethany admitted with a laugh. "The math problem that your sister just showed me is way over my head. Mind giving it a go? I know you have your own crap to do—"

"No problem."

"Thank you, thank you, thank you," Julia repeated, heading back to her seat. Just then Bethany's computer chimed, and she went to settle back on her recliner.

"Wow! Finally pulled out her laptop, I see," Jessica teased.

"Oh, hush and help your sister!" Bethany chastised lightly. She picked up her computer and the response that came back was to the point.

Not to be a purveyor of doom, but you may consider making an appointment with a doctor, one who can refer you to a neurologist. My sister used to have the type of blackouts and headaches you're talking about. She had a tumor in her brain. Fortunately, turned out to be benign. Had it removed and she's right as rain now. Better even. And her irrational anger issues have all but subsided.

Bethany sat back, her mouth agape. All these years she felt herself slipping away, tugging harder after each lapse to return to level-headed rationale. Could this truly be the reason why?

I'm sincerely grateful for your reply and that your sister came through okay, better for her experience. I will definitely see about making an appointment with a doctor.

It was likely she'd get further responses on her chat later, but knew, for now, she would be unable to

digest anything further, so she closed the chat and
pulled up her own video game to play. She loved Sniper
Elite and the latest version she'd purchased recently was
a challenging diversion. While it was loading, she
glanced up and saw her daughters, heads bent in
concentration, working on Julia's homework. Katie,
seated next to them, her headphones on, swaying lightly
to whichever song she was listening to, was clicking
steadily on her keyboard. She smiled and then put on
her own headphones. Tomorrow, she'd call and
schedule an appointment with her general practitioner
and if anything was going on in her brain, she'd tackle it
head on—for her daughters' sakes.

Chapter twenty-three

Bethany awoke the next morning, saw her daughters off and then settled at her desk. She immediately logged into her Kaiser account and scheduled an appointment to see her practitioner at his earliest availability. She concluded that and was set to log into her chat when a knock sounded at the door.

She cursed beneath her breath for forgetting to print out a no-soliciting sign to hang up on her door. With a frustrated sigh, she went to the living room and pulled back the curtain to peer out. Two men in suits stood on her porch, leading her to believe that a pair of Jehovah's Witnesses had come calling, but when the taller of the two spotted her at the window, he held up a badge.

She lowered the curtain and immediately began drawing in deep, calming breaths.

"You aren't here about one of my daughters, are you?" she breathed nervously, the moment she pulled open her front door. "Just tell me they are all okay."

"Um, we're not here about your daughters," Wilson stated, and saw her visibly wilt in relief before his eyes. The fact that she was so concerned over the welfare of her children made him doubt that this woman could be a killer.

"There has been a string of killings recently," Hardwick stated, maintaining distance between his professionalism and his emotions, which too had him doubting whether a woman who cared so greatly for her offspring could be a cold-blooded killer.

"Are you saying I need to be concerned? That I need to be locking my doors?" Bethany asked, the fear in her tone real. To the detectives, her fear sounded justified as a woman concerned for her safety and that of her family. In reality, her fear stemmed from the fact that they were detectives, that they were investigating a string of murders, and they were standing on her doorstep. Her mind was in turmoil and her heart was thudding so loudly against her ribcage that she could barely hear the detective's next words.

"No, Mrs. Barnstead."

How do they know my name? They couldn't possibly know...

"We're going around interviewing people—" Hardwick started, but Bethany interrupted him.

"I'm afraid I don't have any information that could help you."

"The interviews are to do with a specific group of people, not what they may or may not have seen. We're requesting that you come down to the station with us so that we can eliminate you from our inquiries," Wilson stated, feeling awkward. They'd racked their brains yesterday evening, trying to determine the best method in which to get their suspects, of which they had little-to-no evidence against, into the station so that they could pry them with questions in the hopes of getting them to trip themselves up—questions which they hoped wouldn't spur them to lawyer up. Or to get them to willingly give a DNA sample—again, hoping they wouldn't lawyer up. It had been a long night of debates over which tactic they felt would gain the most positive results.

Thus far, their luck had held, and of the six total suspects, three had already agreed to come in to assist with their investigations, especially if it meant 'clearing up any suspicion' about themselves.

"I'm sorry, I'm a little confused," Bethany said, with a slight shake of her head. "You're requesting that I come down to the station so that you can do what again?"

"We're interviewing a select group of individuals in relation to a string of murders that took place recently. We're hoping to gain the cooperation of these individuals so that we might put to rest any involvement one or more of them may have had in these incidents," Hardwick stated, his tone clipped and quick. He hoped that if he remained vague in their expectations, he could hoodwink her into compliance as he had the others.

They could outright lie to them, which wasn't against the law, but after arguing with his fellow detectives for nearly an hour the evening before, they came to an agreement that instead of telling an out-and-out lie, they would, instead, tiptoe around the reasons, vague in their information. Even though it had worked on three people thus far, Hardwick could see the gears turning in this suspect's head. She wasn't falling for it.

"Can I see your badges again?" She asked, her eyes squinting slightly in suspicion. They held up their badges for her to inspect. "Just hold those there for a minute please. Thank you." She pulled her cell phone from her pocket and dialed the non-emergency number. "Hi, yes, um, I have two men here claiming to be detectives, but they don't appear to know precisely what it is they want so I'm just trying to confirm they actually work...yes, um...badge numbers are 62874 and 17122. Your names, please?"

"I'm Detective Stephen Hardwick and this is my colleague, Detective Theodore Wilson."

"Thank you for your time," Bethany said as soon as their identities had been confirmed. "So, detectives, I still don't know precisely what it is that brought you to my door, but I will say that I will not be accompanying you anywhere. I hope that you discover what it is you're searching for, however. Have a lovely evening." Bethany closed the door and then ran to the window to ensure they were leaving. She peered from the curtain, careful not to draw it back to a noticeable level and watched as they climbed into their vehicle.

As soon as they'd pulled out of her driveway, she dashed to her desktop computer, turned it on, then pulled out her SanDisk external hard drive from the bottom drawer of her desk. She plugged it in, and started removing only that information that she considered innocuous as well as of utmost importance to her: pictures and her manuscripts. The rest could go. Once she completed that, she opened File Shredder. Her heart was racing as she started the program running. She then went to her laptop, plugged in the external hard drive, and repeated the process. It would take hours to scrub both systems and then restore each to its basic operating system, but unless the detectives returned quickly with a warrant in hand to search those computers, she should be safe enough. Her phone she wasn't concerned over. Even if they got a warrant for that, she never used it to do research she considered suspicious. Just ordinary day-to-day things, like which shampoo ranked best for color-treated hair. The only other thing she ever did was to check her accounts, which she only ever used for bills and safe purchases. For purchases that could be considered suspicious activity, such as when she bought the thallium, she'd use a gift card and then scrubbed her computer and search history. For other purchases, such as her disposable coveralls and taser, she got cash from cash back withdrawals at the grocery store. Although it would be easy for the police to question her cash withdrawals, she only ever pulled out twenty at a time, so that she could prove she'd used that money for lottery tickets, something she purchased regularly. The few times she didn't, she tucked the cash in a cash box, along with money obtained from her bi-annual yard sales. Eventually, it tallied enough to buy the taser and easily covered her disposable coveralls, zip ties, and duct tape.

Caution had become her middle name since marrying Shane, but buying things in cash had become the norm when she found out that her purchase history was readily available for anyone to view if they managed to access her Walmart account online. It had startled her to see a history of her purchases when she'd gone online to shop one afternoon. From then on out, she'd paid cash for anything that could be perceived as suspicious.

Scrubbing her systems, however, was a routine she'd perfected years before. Learning how to scrub her computer was one of the first searches she'd performed when she was a senior in high school because she'd come home to find her mother snooping on her computer. After a fight that had the cops at their door, she'd stormed into her room and immediately pulled up her search engine, learned how to scrub her hard drive and delete her internet search history. The next morning, she'd interviewed for the job of a nanny and moved out shortly after.

In her brief marriage to her first husband, Jimmy, Bethany felt sheltered, but the trauma at the hands of her mom made deleting her search history and regularly scrubbing her computer a habit. Then Shane drove home that need, and she'd increased the frequency with which she scrubbed her systems, never wanting him to discover anything he could use as ammunition against her. She downloaded her manuscripts and photos of her daughters to her external hard drive, safely hidden, the rest she annihilated without a second thought.

While the programs worked to destroy any data on her systems, she set about walking room-to-room, racking her brain on anything she may have forgotten to destroy or get rid of. She felt a calm come over her when she recalled that the only three tools she ever purchased were no more: disposable coveralls—last one used was burned, the rest thrown in a dumpster far away from her house; industrial-strength zip ties—trashed weeks ago in a different dumpster; and duct tape. That last item was tucked in her toolbox, a staple that could be found in any home.

A final thought struck her, and she looked toward the front yard. Her heart suddenly felt as if it stopped beating and she sank to the floor, overcome with immense trepidation: the taser.

Chapter twenty-four

"It's her," Hardwick said as he put the car in reverse and slowly exited the suspect's driveway.

"Why? Because of a hunch? Because she didn't fall for our lame attempts to get her to come down to the precinct? Anyone watching Law & Order or Audit the Audit on YouTube could have easily outwitted us on that. Is it because she's intelligent and well-spoken? She is a self-professed writer. Just because she ticked all our boxes, doesn't prove guilt. And your hunch isn't going to be enough to get us a warrant to search her premises to find the evidence we'll need to put her away because our entire search for her was based on potentially erroneous assumptions that our killer wears coveralls and that they are a writer. So, like it or not, you may be certain, but certainty isn't evidence. And, as of now, we've still got nothing."

"Yeah, and if my hunch is right, we'll have nothing after Cortez and Harding finish interviewing those individuals who did willingly come in."

"If we've got nothing, where do we go from here? We certainly can't force her to come to the station, we can't plant evidence that can get us the warrant we need to search her house—"

"No, but if we have probable cause we can get a warrant."

"There isn't a judge on this planet that's going to give you a warrant based on your gut instinct."

"The captain still has some pull with a few judges, maybe he can use his powers of persuasion—"

"We'd never be able to live with ourselves if we pulled this woman in based on a hunch. You know that as well I do, Hardwick."

"I know. Let's grab some lunch before heading back to the precinct. Harding and Cortez have the interviews well in hand and we're done for now anyway. Besides, I haven't eaten anything since about six-thirty this morning. I'm famished."

"I could eat. What do you have in mind?"

"Chinese? Mexican? McDonalds? You name something, I can find something from there to eat."

"Let's do Chipotle."

"Sounds good. We can pick each other's brains some more. Determine the best way to go about getting evidence against Bethany Barnstead."

"You're really fixated on her, aren't you?"

"Yeah, it's weird I know, but remember earlier when Officer Chavez said that his instincts about her were strong?"

"Are you certain your Spidey senses aren't tingling because of that conversation? Is it possible that you're a bit biased because of what Officer Chavez shared and because she didn't fall for the worm on our hook?"

Hardwick pulled into the Chipotle parking lot, "we'll discuss it more at length after we eat."

An hour and a half later, they headed back to their car, no closer to an idea on how to convince Bethany Barnstead to turn herself in. They both realized that that was just the beginning of their trials when they pulled into the precinct parking lot.

The media had arrived.

Front and center of the pack was one reporter he'd hoped never to meet up with again, and in true fashion, she was yelling at him the moment he parked his vehicle.

"Detective Hardwick, it's Cassandra Bouchard with Channel 5. Can I ask you about the spree killings that took place a few weeks back? Is it true that the killer has gone to ground, and you have no leads?"

Hardwick turned around and strolled over to the reporter, "You always know what to say to stop me in my tracks, don't you, Cassandra? One of these days you are going to have to tell me from where you get your information."

"I got a call from the killer," she answered bluntly, and Hardwick took a step back, shock flitting across his features. He composed himself and stepped up closer to Cassandra, "Would you accompany me inside the station, please?"

"If you expect me to give up my source—" Cassandra started, but Hardwick was already shaking his head.

"I know it would take a court order and a month in jail before you'd even begin to consider something like that, and that's time I don't have to waste. I do, however, want you to fill me in on your phone call…without revealing anything that would break your oath as a reporter, of course," he finished, a twinge of sarcasm in his tone.

Cassandra nodded, "It's one of the reasons I'm here."

"That, and you're hoping for an exclusive, no doubt," Wilson added.

"But of course," she grinned, then turned and headed toward the front door. Her camera person started to follow but Wilson stepped in front of the tagalong, "We only need to speak to Miss Bouchard. You can wait here. She'll be along shortly."

Cassandra nodded her assent, "It's okay, Vikki. I'll call you if I need you to call in the cavalry."

The two detectives walked straight to the captain's office, Cassandra following along behind.

Wilson and Harding had just exited one of the interrogation rooms, spotted the trio, and went after them. The captain saw the horde approaching and immediately headed them off. "With so many of us, I think perhaps we better take this to the conference room. Miss Bouchard, lovely to see you again. Have a seat," Captain Parsons said amiably. "So, what brings you to the precinct?"

"She got a call from the killer," Hardwick said, his tone grim.

The captain sighed, "so we do have another glory seeker on our hands then?" A quick glance at his detectives and he knew that all their minds jumped straight to Christian Price. None spoke his name, however.

"What took them so long to contact the media, I wonder?" Cortez asked rhetorically.

"Yeah, why do you think they took so long to get in touch and is it true that the person has stopped their spree killing for now?" Cassandra asked in true reporter fashion.

"We're not ready for media coverage yet, Cassandra—"

"But I'll be the one you call when you are ready?"

"Absolutely, but why don't you tell us what the killer said to you—"

"—and no doubt to every reporter currently outside," Wilson added.

"It was short and to the point. He stated—"

"He?" Cortez interrupted.

"Could've been a she, but the pitch of the voice, which sounded as if it was being spoken through a filter of some sort, made me think male."

Hardwick immediately started rubbing his forehead and breathing heavily through his nostrils.

Cassandra continued, "He…or she…said that there had been five deaths committed in a very short span a few weeks ago and that the police were on a fishing expedition because there was no evidence to link anyone to the crimes. Is that true?"

The captain chewed at his bottom lip, his breathing also growing more pronounced. "Will you excuse me for a few minutes, Cassandra. Harding, can I speak to you out in the hall?"

"Sure thing, Captain."

After a few minutes, the captain returned, minus Harding. Without preamble, he stated, "What I can tell you is that, yes, we had five kills. Two in one week, followed by three more a week later in the span of one night. Now, nothing for the last three weeks."

His detectives were looking at him, wide-eyed, disbelief written all over their faces. Never had the captain so willingly provided details to a reporter on an open case. Especially in which there were no leads to provide, and one which made them look incompetent.

"So, knowing the heinous manner of the crimes," the captain continued, "would you be willing to give us the name and/or number of the person who called you?"

Cassandra shook her head, "Blocked number. No name given. So, you have zero leads to go on?"

The captain sighed again, "would you be willing to allow our techs to go—"

"Not in a million years," Cassandra interjected sharply. "Look, I came in here as a professional courtesy. To let you know that your killer has been in contact with the media. I didn't have to do that, but I did because I respect what you guys are up against."

"Then help us by letting us see your phone records," Hardwick implored again.

"My first amendment rights as a journalist may be limited, but you know you can't compel me to reveal my source."

"But this isn't really a source, is it Miss Bouchard," Wilson stated. "This was a call from a killer. One that didn't provide a name—so, no source information there. Not only that, but it's also not someone with whom you rely on regularly for information that you use to compose your stories so that you can provide honest news of legitimate public importance. Right now, this was a one-off call from a murdering psychopath who just wanted to get her rocks off by taunting the police. So, I'd say your first amendment rights wouldn't be trampled on if you wanted to help us stop him…or her. And since we're just asking you for a telephone number, you wouldn't really be giving up too much information."

Cassandra glared at Hardwick, "you assured me that you wouldn't try to compel me to give up my source if I came in here to speak to you."

Hardwick nodded, "I did, yes. I did that because the likelihood of getting information from you, even if compelled, could take months and we really don't have months. It really isn't my goal—or that of this department—to see you jailed, Cassandra. As always, our goal is simply to put a killer away, and right now, like it or not, you're our best hope of doing that."

Just then Harding returned with a flushed, mildly overweight man in close pursuit. The captain recognized him and immediately went over to shake his hand.

"The is highly unorthodox, Gary, and well you know it."

"I know, but I appreciate you racing over here, nonetheless," the captain expressed. "Did Harding fill you in en route?"

"He did, and I must say, I'm really not pleased about all of this. Miss Bouchard," he greeted tersely.

"Judge Carmichael," she greeted, equally terse. The judge turned to face the captain again, "It's just a good thing that Detective Harding caught me between cases, or you wouldn't be getting this favor from me, Gary." He turned again to Cassandra, "It's my understanding that you have information that could lead to the identity of a spree killer, Miss Bouchard?"

"How in Hell could you possibly…" she stopped speaking and glared at Harding. "Captain Parsons sent you after the judge because he knew that I wouldn't willingly give up any information related to my source. Well, judge or not, I don't have to say another damned word." Cassandra pressed her lips together and sat, stiff and unresponsive.

"I'm not here to stamp on your first amendment rights, so let's get that straight right off the bat," the judge continued, "however, you know that in exigent circumstances I can request that you reveal your source when there is probable cause to believe that the information you have is relevant to a specific violation of the law, which it is. Unless you do not believe that murder is a violation of the law?"

Cassandra simply sat, glaring, which the judge ignored. "Since I believe, based on the information provided, that there is cause for you to reveal certain pertinent information—"

"I don't know the name of the source," Cassandra reiterated sharply.

"Revelation of the source can come in different ways, not simply by providing a name. Do you have a way in which these detectives can find your source?"

"We need to go through her phone records," the captain piped up. "See if we can get a lead on what she states is a blocked number."

"Detective Harding, follow me back to my chambers and I'll provide you with a warrant to search Miss Bouchard's phone records."

"You can't do that!" Cassandra yelled. "There isn't sufficient cause for a warrant—"

"Sufficient enough in my books," the judge said, then stood and headed out of the precinct. This time with Harding chasing up the rear.

"I'll be filing a complaint with the judiciary commission!" Cassandra called and then pulled out her phone. She dialed Vikki, "send in the cavalry."

Chapter twenty-five

Bethany wasn't certain what she was going to do, but she only waited ten minutes after the detectives left her house to act. The first thing she did was to drive to Walmart and purchase another pay-as-you-go phone. The first she'd purchased in a 'just in case' scenario and ended up using it to call the ambulance for one of those victimized people she aided. That phone had been tossed in a dumpster well away from her home. Now, she needed another one.

She'd researched these extensively when preparing to write one of her books, so she was aware she needed to use caution. Burner phones were traceable…at least the number was. But the only way it would trace back to her is if she registered it—which she never did—or if she used it to make personal calls along with the anonymous calls that she intended to make to the press. Basically, buy a burner phone for its intended purpose, use it for that intended purpose only, and dispose of it immediately after.

To ensure that anyone surveilling her didn't get suspicious, she purchased groceries also, withdrew her twenty dollars cash back, then made a second stop at the 7-11 convenience store to purchase her weekly lottery ticket. All the while behaving as if detectives from the Atlanta Police Department hadn't paid her a visit that morning; behaving as if those very same detectives were following her every move.

The only qualms she had about this part of her plan was that her nonchalance after being visited by the police might make her appear psychologically imbalanced. After all, a normal person might not think to run errands right after being all but accused of committing murder. Since she couldn't think of another way around it, she figured this was her best bet.

She went home and pulled up her computer, then searched for the numbers of three of the local news stations. She then erased her search history, collected her purse, and headed back out. Again, she only prayed that no one was tailing her, but she needed the media to distract the police so that she could find a safe place to dispose of her taser—and the disposable phone once she actually turned it on and used it.

She glanced at her watch. It was still before lunch time, which gave her a few hours before the girls came home. She had a single-minded goal to accomplish and was grateful to have the time to do it. Careful to stick to the back roads, she took the short jaunt to I-75, constantly checking her rearview mirror to ensure she wasn't being followed, then accelerated into traffic, putting her foot down, she wove in and out, watching her rearview to spot any taggers. When she felt assured that there weren't any, she moved back into the righthand lane and began looking at the blue directional highway signs that would indicate a park.

A quick glance at her fuel gauge had her turning off the next exit since she was down to a quarter of a tank and didn't know just how much longer she would need to drive. So, she took the off-ramp for North Marietta Parkway. Surprisingly, there wasn't a gas station in sight, but what did appear was a sign for Merritt Park. She turned into the small lot and immediately began scanning for security cameras; sighing with relief when she didn't spot any.

The parking lot was empty of cars, so she pulled into one closest to the tennis court and scanned the park itself. The restroom and tennis court restricted much of her view, which meant that if anyone were on the green, they'd likely not see her either. Not that she expected to see anyone midday on a workday.

Bethany pulled the disposable phone from her purse then followed the steps to activate it. Once it was ready to use, she pulled out her winter scarf and wrapped it around the mouthpiece. When someone answered, she dropped the timber of her voice as deep as it would go, "I have a news story for one of your reporters."

She repeated this for each of the numbers called and then relayed only a few details about the murders before hanging up. The last thing she needed was for one of them to develop a sudden moral conscience and notify the police who could then put a trace on her number and track her down before she finished what she started.

As soon as the third call was finished, she pried open the back panel of the phone and removed the SIM card, then drove as close to the trash bin as she could and tossed the phone out the window. It clanked loudly as it struck the bin, but she'd landed the toss. Even if they tracked the number to that park and found the cell phone, she was wearing gloves, so they'd never be able to pull fingerprints off it. Likely a trash worker would find the phone and sell it on Craigslist. Next, she hurled the SIM card into the grass, knowing that the tiny piece of electronics would never be found.

Satisfied she'd accomplished one of her goals and there would be no one to trace anything back to her, she set her thoughts on her second goal: getting rid of her taser. She didn't think that the prongs in each gun were uniquely identifiable, but it wasn't a risk she wanted to take if they discovered she owned one. She'd thought about taking it to a pawn shop but that thought was fleeting. Definitely security cameras there.

She wished that she lived near enough to a lake or river. There was a small pond in Capital Gateway Park, but that was way too close to her home for comfort. She could just envision that scenario: killer incapacitating with a taser, a taser gets found by some local kids in the pond, police—already suspicious of her as the killer—pay her another visit with a search warrant. No, no waterways near to her home would do, and she couldn't risk doing a search for any either because all she had on her was her cellphone and if they managed to get a warrant for that...no, her best option was to simply drive until an opportunity presented itself.

She headed back to I-75, then stopped to fill up her tank at the next available exit before heading up I-575. She spotted a turnoff for the Sweetwater day-use area at Lake Allatoona and headed that way, grinning. Driving along Kellogg Creek Road, she was elated to see a bridge coming up. She grabbed the taser, checked for traffic behind and in front of her, and was fairly laughing aloud when she reached the center of the bridge and hurled the taser into the water below. She continued to drive a short distance before turning around and heading the thirty minutes back home.

She pulled into her driveway feeling safer and happier than she had in a long while, knowing that she was now untouchable—unless they managed to get a warrant for her DNA, which they couldn't do without probable cause. "Which they will never have." She glanced at her watch, "I still have time for a late lunch before the girls get home." She climbed from her vehicle, went to check her mail, and spotted an unmarked sedan pulling to a stop a few doors down.

Chapter twenty-six

"Do you think the attorney will be able to overturn the judge's warrant?" Wilson queried.

"Considering that Cassandra is yelling loud enough to be heard outside the closed door, I'd say that answer is a resounding no," Harding quipped.

"She's gonna make minced meat out of us on her next news broadcast," Cortez grinned.

"We did what we had to do," Hardwick said shortly.

Less than ten minutes after he arrived, the attorney walked out of the conference room, glaring at the detectives, "Miss Bouchard will give you the phone number that called her phone. Since that's the only contact she's had with the perpetrator and since she's already willingly conveyed everything relayed to her by said perpetrator, there shouldn't be any reason to enforce the warrant and pull her records." Without another word, the attorney turned and stormed from the precinct.

"Thank you," Harding said to the now empty space. "That'll save us loads of time in bringing this killer to justice. You get that, right, you asshole? You get that we're trying to stop a killer?"

"Um, you okay, *jefe*? You do realize that he's gone, right?"

Harding shook in head in exasperation, "Yeah, I'm good. Just sick to death of reporters yanking the police around in the name of the first amendment. Hell, I'm all for the first amendment, but I certainly wouldn't put my first amendment right above the lives of other people. That's just straight up arrogance."

"Well, since the news station's attorney agrees that I need to be cooperative," Cassandra said as she approached, her tone spewing disagreement, "here's the phone number that I got the call from."

"So, not a blocked number," Hardwick snorted, handing the paper over to Cortez. "Get it traced."

Cassandra shrugged, "For what it's worth, I do hope you catch 'em."

"That's always the plan."

"Yeah, but things don't always go according to plan, do they, detective?"

"You planning to run the story tonight?"

"That's not up to me, it's up to the producer. I'll pass on the information…wait…you aren't going to ask me to hold off, are you? Because after what happened here today, there's no way in Hell—"

"No, I'm going to ensure you have all the facts correct. You're getting your exclusive on a silver platter," Hardwick stated.

266

"Well, at least the news anchors will," Cassandra huffed as she followed the detective to his desk.

"Then let's ensure that it'll be written in news-worthy fashion, shall we?"

"You're going to help me write a news report?" Cassandra laughed.

"Hey, don't laugh. I write up reports every day."

Cassandra knew he was trying to lighten the tension, but he couldn't hide the anger in his stride which was nearly palpable. She truly felt for him because she knew all too well how difficult his job was. Her dad had been a cop, killed in the line of duty, so she wasn't without sympathy. She'd also tagged along after this particular detective enough to know that his reaction to this killer was becoming a near personal vendetta, much as it had with the Christian Price case.

"You may not catch him...or her. You probably know the statistics better than I do, but I've done a news story or two about murder and—"

"Five- to ten-thousand murders go unsolved, nationwide, every year," Hardwick finished.

"Then why do you continually feel the need to beat yourself up so badly when one gets away? Even I know you put your all into every case that comes across your desk. Well, not personally, but I've witnessed that drive of yours, so I don't believe I'm far off the mark.

267

Still, if one gets dropped into the cold case files, I truly believe it isn't because of a lack of effort on your part, or the detectives you work with."

Hardwick chewed on his bottom lip as if doing all he could to hold back a retort. Instead, he sucked in a deep breath and pulled out the file on victim number one.

Later that evening, he turned on the television for the six o'clock news. He didn't often watch the news but tonight he wanted to make certain that the report he and Cassandra worked on earlier that day was broadcast, praying that the news anchors didn't muck it up with rewrites, as Cassandra suggested they might do.

His cellphone rang, "Hardwick."

"It's Cassandra Bouchard, detective. I just wanted to call to let you know that—"

Cassandra, you're on in five!

"I can't talk long. The producer has me on with the news anchors tonight. I'll be presenting the story at the anchor desk."

"Congrats. I know that's the aspiration of field reporters everywhere."

"Yeah, it's a big deal, but I didn't call to brag. I called to let you know that I'll deliver the message. I'll make certain it gets heard."

"Much appreciated, Cassandra. Oh…I'll be watching tonight."

"Great, now my anxiety just shot through the roof."

Hardwick snorted, "You'll do fine."

"Thanks, Detective. Gotta run."

Hardwick placed his cellphone on the coffee table and walked to the kitchen for a beer. After all, the person in the background had shouted that he had five minutes before Cassandra would be on. He'd just settled onto the sofa again when the anchor introduced Cassandra.

We're joined tonight by one of our field reporters, Cassandra Bouchard. How are you this evening, Cassandra?

Couldn't be better, Pete. Thank you for the opportunity to personally bring this story to you tonight.

Hardwick snorted, "Not that he had a choice in the matter."

We understand that you had a bit of a harrowing experience with our local law enforcement today. Is that right?

Well, Cecilia, I don't know if I'd call it harrowing, but it's never easy, going toe-to-toe with the APD's finest, let me tell you. They are a seriously dedicated group of detectives over at Zone 5, and for them to give me a firsthand account of what happened in our fine city a few weeks ago…well, that's what was harrowing.

Cassandra turned from her colleagues to face the camera, *Before I begin, I would like to warn our viewers that the details of this are horrific, as are the images that we've obtained from the detectives working on these cases. Five of Atlanta's citizens were brutally murdered in the span of two weeks, three in one horrifying night.* Images given to Cassandra of the crime scenes were indeed horrific. Even Hardwick, who'd viewed them time and again, glanced away briefly, especially when the chaotic scene from victim two flashed up. *The killer, known only by her signature, Seeker of Justice, was out to serve up justice to abusers around the city, but the APD need her, and others like her, to know that it's their job to bring people to justice. That we cannot condone vigilantism for any reason, because if we allow people to kill for every perceived wrong…well, they themselves could get it wrong and kill an innocent person. Were these targets innocent? That should've been for a jury of their peers to decide. If you suspect someone you love is being abused, please call the police non-emergency line, unless there is an imminent threat to life or limb. To Seeker of Justice, the APD have a message for you: they have your number, your blood, and are actively collecting the evidence they need to put you away. If you, yourself, were a victim of abuse, let them get you the help you need.*

Hardwick clicked off the television and laid his head against the back of his sofa. He didn't even know whether the killer would see the news broadcast, only hoped that she did, and something would strike the right nerve, reach deep inside her psychopathic soul so to cause her to turn herself in.

Chapter twenty-seven

Bethany wasn't watching the news. Instead, she was making a concerted effort to pay attention to her daughters and not get up to watch the car parked down the street. Instinct told her that she was being surveilled, which let her know that she was more than a person of interest in the killings, she was a suspect. What she was having difficulty wrapping her brain around, was how. What had the detectives discovered that led them to her door? Even if they found her blood at the scene of her final kill, that wouldn't tell them her name and address, so how did she even get on their radar?

The sound of her daughters' laughter drew her back to her living room and out of her own thoughts. Her thoughts were a place she didn't need to go, because it tended to be a dark, scary place. She focused on her daughters instead.

It was a rare evening when all of them were home at the same time. Most times they were at the library studying, in classes, at work, or hanging out with friends.

"I was planning to cook dinner, but it's been ages since we've gone out together as a family—" Bethany started but Katie interrupted.

"Why don't we go down to Café Bourbon. We haven't been there in years."

"You mean you'd prefer that to McDonalds?" Bethany asked in exaggerated shock.

The girls laughed, but then Tanya piped up, "We don't have to walk, do we? It's dark and cold outside."

"No, we'll drive."

"Can we do BBQ instead? I've got a craving for BBQ," Jessica piped up.

"That's because you like the guy working over at Hattie Marie's," Katie teased.

"I do not," Jessica huffed.

"I do believe the woman doth protest too much," Julia giggled.

"I just want BBQ."

"We can do BBQ," Bethany laughed. "It's only a 15-minute drive."

"Awesome. Who wants to ride with me?" Jessica asked, jumping up to grab her car keys. She'd scrimped and saved over the summer to purchase herself an inexpensive first ride and was thrilled when she'd passed her driver's test on the first go. The twin's enthusiastic acceptance made Katie look sadly at her mom, "I'll ride with you, Mom."

"It's fine if you want to ride with your sisters. We'll meet up in no time."

"You sure?"

"Absolutely."

Everyone headed out the front door and piled into Jessica's car. Bethany smiled and climbed into her Oldsmobile, fired up the engine, and pulled out of the driveway before Jessica even started her car. She'd done it on purpose because she needed to see if that car was still there, needed to ease her mind if she was to keep her focus on her girls this evening.

She breathed an audible sigh when she didn't see the vehicle, but her nerves jumped when she spotted headlights turn on in her rearview mirror and a car start toward her.

"Could be just a neighbor, Bethany. You really need to relax and just breathe," She chastised herself, then glanced in her rearview mirror again, and saw Jessica's car pull onto the road behind the other car. Within fifteen minutes, Bethany pulled into the parking lot of Hattie Marie's.

The car drove past, and Bethany's pulse slowed. She greeted her daughters at their car when Jessica pulled to a stop. As usual, their laughter filled the air as they opened their doors and got out. She couldn't help but shake her head and smile at them. Her smile faded, when she spotted a familiar figure walking up the street toward the BBQ place.

It took her but a split second to recognize the man who'd come to her door a few weeks earlier,

274

feigning—she now knew—as someone working for Labor Statistics. She told the girls to go in and get them a table and then walked over to intercept the officer.

"I'll have your name and badge number," she said succinctly.

The officer hesitated briefly, but then reached in and pulled out a card with his information on it.

"Thank you. Enjoy the BBQ. It really is some of the best around. As for me, I'm going to go and enjoy the company of my children. Have a good evening, Officer."

Chapter twenty-eight

A week after his encounter with Bethany Barnstead outside of the BBQ joint, Officer Chavez walked around the detective desks and straight to the captain's office. He was chagrined to see all the detectives on the Seeker of Justice case in there with him. Captain Parsons glanced up and nodded, "meet us in the conference room, Officer. We'll be along in a few minutes."

"I know you aren't going to like this, Hardwick, but we haven't got anything. No justification to keep manpower on this case. I'm calling it—"

"Can we just see why she filed a complaint against Officer Chavez first?"

"Really Hardwick? Dragging out the inevitable, aren't you?" Harding queried, shaking his head. "The woman made all the right moves. If she played chess, she'd be on par with Judit Polgár…and yes, I play chess, so pick your jaws up off the floor."

"Chill, *jefe*, I can see why Hardwick is hesitant to put this one to bed. I mean, we know who did this, we even have her blood—"

"—we just can't prove it," Wilson finished. "Without her DNA on file and no way to get a warrant to compel a DNA sample to compare to the blood left at the scene, we've got bupkis."

"Okay, we've already been round and round on this, so let's put it on the backburner and just go see what Chavez has to say for himself." The captain stood and followed his detectives to the conference room. "I'll get right to the point, Officer," the captain started before everyone was seated, "why would Bethany Barnstead file a case of harassment against you?"

"Did you really take it upon yourself to tail her?" Harding asked, his tone impressed.

Officer Chavez had the good sense to look embarrassed, but then jutted his chin out in defiance, "I had a hunch and I wanted to prove that my gut instinct was correct. She's guilty and we all know she's guilty."

"Yeah, but if you'd discovered any signs of guilt, you'd have been in here like a flash sharing your findings, wouldn't you?" the captain asked.

The officer nodded, "She's good, I'll give her that. I managed to tail her a good while the morning after Detectives Hardwick and Wilson visited her house—"

"You were there?" Hardwick asked, shocked.

Officer Chavez grinned, "Yes, sir. And within a few minutes of you leaving, she was off. At first, it appeared as if she was just running errands, but soon after making a trek to Walmart, she was off again. I managed to keep up with her while she was racing down

I-75, but then she unexpectedly took the North Marietta Parkway off ramp, and I lost track of her."

"Wait! Did you say North Marietta Parkway?" Hardwick stood suddenly when Chavez nodded. He raced out of the conference room and straight to his desk, rooting through the files strewn across the surface. "Come on, come on…gotcha!" He picked up the file and with a cockiness to his stride, he placed it on the table in front of the captain, "You may want to hold off closing the book on this one."

Chapter twenty-nine

Bethany sat on her vanity stool, staring at her reflection in the mirror, the shock of her results from the contrast MRI, earlier that morning, made her head hurt. The doctor had done all he could to appear sympathetic when she'd gone in to discuss those results, but instead came off sounding patronizing.

"You may want to get your affairs in order," he'd said, his bland, unaffected tone grating on her nerves. There she sat looking at the image of a malignant tumor pressing against her frontal lobe and for a long while found herself at a loss for words.

Finally, she managed to croak out 'how long?' and felt a tremor of fear race through her body at his response so callously delivered: *I can't say with any certainty, but…maybe a couple of weeks, a month at most.* After five minutes more of numbed silence on her part, he quietly departed the room with a 'I'll leave you to your thoughts'.

A nurse arrived a few minutes later with brochures in hand: *Radiation Therapy for Brain Tumors* and *No One Should Have to Fight Cancer Alone.*

She glanced down at those two informational pamphlets now in stunned silence. According to the doctor, she could try radiation, but the tumor had metastasized, and it may not prove beneficial at this late stage.

Her biggest concern now, as she stared at her reflection again, was how to break the news to her daughters. She had no doubt that Jessica and Katie would do all they could to care for their fifteen-year-old twin sisters, but at only eighteen, she didn't know if the state would allow that to happen.

No matter, she would write up a document requesting that the girls not be separated. After that, all that remained for her to do was to ensure that Jessica was named as beneficiary on all her accounts and to go to the courthouse as soon as possible, so she could deed the house into their names. Her mind started making a list of things she needed to do, agencies the girls would need to contact, and arrangements for after she passed. Her logic circuits kicked on and she immediately wrote down 'direct cremation' on one of the pamphlets. The last thing she wanted or needed was for the girls to use what funds remained in her account on an expensive funeral, but nonetheless, she would ultimately leave it up to them to decide what to do.

A knock at the door interrupted her thoughts. She stood wearily and opened it straight away, which was contrary to her normally cautious nature of checking from behind the curtain first.

If she was shocked to see the two detectives on her doorstep, it didn't show on her face.

"Can I help you, detectives?" she asked quietly. Her mind was too preoccupied to care one whit about their intentions. They could be there to notify her that she was to be electrocuted tomorrow for her crimes, and it wouldn't phase her. But she did care enough about her daughters not to do anything foolish—like blurt out that she was guilty of the crimes they were there to discuss with her. Instinctively, she glanced at her watch: nine o'clock a.m. Good, her children wouldn't be home for a long time yet. Of late, that was her primary concern—would her children be present to witness something that she didn't want them to know about?

"Good morning, Mrs. Barnstead," Detective Wilson opened, "there's a matter of great importance we'd like to discuss with you, if we may. Preferably down at the station."

If Bethany wasn't so dejected by the events of the morning already, she'd have grinned at the obvious ploy to get her to come with them willingly, no doubt to try to subvert the course of justice by asking her a barrage of questions in an attempt to trip her up, to get her to confess her crimes, or to trick her into giving up her DNA. If they had something on her, they'd simply arrest her. Still, it wouldn't hurt to confirm her suspicions.

"Am I under arrest?" she asked softly.

"No ma'am." Hardwick nearly choked on that denial wanting instead to pull out the handcuffs and haul her to the station in the back of his police car.

"If you'll provide me the address of the station, I'll be there within the hour." Bethany took the proffered card and slowly closed the door.

Hardwick and Wilson stood a moment longer, staring at the front door in confusion.

"Well, that didn't go as anticipated," Wilson said finally, turning to head back to the car. Hardwick stood a moment longer, then followed. "I half expected her to sic her dog on us."

"Did you notice something off about her?"

"We've only met her the one other time," Wilson declared.

"In person, maybe, but wouldn't you say we've gotten to know her through her notes left at the crime scene?"

"The psychotic part of her, sure," Wilson snorted. "But this is only our second face-to-face—"

"And you don't see a massive difference in the woman we met that first time and the woman we spoke to just now?" Hardwick persisted.

"Somehow, I feel that if I say no, it's going to be the wrong answer," Wilson quipped. When Hardwick rolled his eyes, Wilson grinned. "No, sorry. Seriously, I did, yes. There was a depressive cloud hanging over her head."

"Do you think she'll show at the station in an hour? Like she said?"

"Maybe…if she doesn't commit suicide first."

Detective Hardwick's gaze widened as he stared at his partner across the roof of their car, "son of a bitch," he muttered, then ran back up the driveway and up to the front door. Without hesitation, he started banging loudly.

Chapter thirty

Bethany tossed the detective's business card onto her coffee table, then went straight to the bathroom to shower. She shed her clothes, trying hard to push down the nervous tension welling in her stomach over going down to the precinct.

She turned on the shower, then found her favorite playlist on YouTube music, set it to playing loudly through her Bluetooth speakers, then climbed in. Immediately, she sat down and let the water spray across her naked body, praying it would wash away the feelings of hopelessness saturating her very soul.

Zeus set to barking a minute later, which brought her out of her doldrums just long enough to shout at him to quiet down, then she laid her head on her knees and let the tears fall. In her estimation, she'd spent too many of her thirty-nine years either crying or repressing her emotions. It was no wonder cancer had managed to gain a foothold in her brain.

The intrusion of Detective Hardwick into her bathroom was an unexpected jolt and she was irrationally grateful that she was sitting with her knees drawn, when he yanked back the shower door.

"What in the name of all that is holy do you think you are doing?" she screeched, drawing her knees tighter against her chest.

Hardwick just stood there, gawking for a minute, and then spun around.

"Get the hell out of my bathroom and out of my house, you son-of-a-bitch!" she screamed when he still hadn't moved.

He bolted from the bathroom, leaving a stunned Bethany to close the shower door on her own. Any pity-party feelings she had regarding her condition fled as a deep-seated rage consumed her.

She stood up, turned off the shower, grabbed her towel and went to get dressed. They wanted her at the station, well, they were going to get her at the station sooner than they anticipated, and more than ready to do battle.

"Invade my home like that, you arrogant toad!" she ranted, yanking on her undergarments. "I'll give you what for the likes of which you ain't never seen in your life."

Hardwick walked stiffly from the house to the car where Wilson was waiting with a massive grin on his face, "I take it that she didn't commit suicide?"

"Just go!"

"Do you think she'll still come to the station after you strolled into her house—"

"You made me think she was suicidal," Hardwick snapped.

"That's because I did think she could be suicidal, but from the sound of the screeching coming from the house at your invasion, I'd say we were both wrong. Hopefully, that won't prevent her from coming to talk to us."

"Oh, I think she'll be there with bells on—"

"—and an attorney in tow?"

"No, I think she'll want to rub our faces in just how smart she is."

"Maybe she'll cool off once you apologize to her," Wilson goaded.

"Just get us back to the station so we can prepare for her arrival, which I have a feeling will be soon after we get back."

Hardwick wasn't far off the mark. Bethany appeared at the station within five minutes after the detectives, but if they expected her to be foaming at the mouth, they were wrong because she was downright calm. Scary calm.

Of course, she'd spent her entire drive over doing her Zen breathing and pushing her emotions deep down into her core. She reminded herself that she'd not allowed anyone to get the emotional upper hand with her and she wasn't about to let that change now.

She was here to listen to what they had to say and nothing more. Once she left the precinct, she would move on with what time she had left. That would be her sole focus.

"Ms. Barnstead, I want to apologize to you for the intrusion—" Hardwick went to greet her when she was shown into the detective's space.

Bethany's grinned grimly, "I admit that I was shocked and rather dismayed at having you invade my private space. May I ask what caused you to—"

"I…I mean…we…my partner and I…well, we were concerned for your wellbeing," Hardwick stammered.

"What Detective Hardwick is trying to say," Wilson interjected, moving to stand next to his partner, "is that your demeanor was such that when we departed, we immediately worried that you may do something…foolish."

"Like kill myself?" Bethany did laugh then, albeit it was more of a short guffaw. "Well, I guess I should be thanking you for caring about my wellbeing so wholeheartedly then. Where would you like to conduct this interview that you spoke of?"

"This way," Hardwick turned and headed to the conference room, his mind fighting to maintain its balance. This woman's level of emotional detachment bordered on menacing. Not half an hour ago, she was numb and depressed, then was crying and screaming in rage and now she was cool as a cucumber. If he doubted her to be a psychopath before, his doubt was fleeing rapidly. That made him doubt that she would crack under the pressure of their questions.

"Have a seat. Can I get you a drink?"

"No, I'm good. Thank you." Bethany sat with her hands in her lap, refusing to touch any surface in the room. There wasn't a record of her DNA on file, and she didn't intend for there to be a record of her fingerprints either. "So, what is that you and Detective Wilson wish to discuss?"

Hardwick decided not to play cat and mouse with her since she was expecting that, instead he got straight to the point. "Last week, Officer Chavez followed you around for a bit—"

"Ah, the unauthorized surveillance that I needed to file a complaint about. I do hope that was satisfactorily resolved and that Officer Chavez won't take it upon himself to tail someone again who's committed no crime."

Hardwick ignored what he perceived to be a rhetorical question and continued his line of inquiry, "He followed you up I-75 to North Marietta Parkway. May I inquire as to what took you up there on that morning?"

"You may inquire." Bethany said but offered nothing further. In her mind, she was grinning. She'd watched too many attorneys speaking on the 'worse type of defendant to interrogate' and they all agreed it was those who offered up zero details, zero information; those who merely answered the questions as they were asked—no more, no less. The best defendants from a prosecutorial point of view were those who loved to talk because they were the ones who tended to offer up more details than asked for, which, in turn, provided the rope needed to hang themselves.

"It just so happens that we were able to trace a telephone number from that vicinity on the same morning that you went for your drive to that area," Wilson added, but Bethany remained silent, her face emotionless.

"It was from that number that three calls were placed to the local media related to the Seeker of Justice murders," Hardwick prodded, hoping that the use of her own signature would cause some form of reaction. He wanted to scream when no recognition lit her gaze. "That caller provided details to the media about five brutal killings that took place a little over a month ago, all within the span of two weeks."

In true crime fashion, Wilson began pulling out the crime scene photos and spreading them out on the table in front of Bethany.

"Don't you want to look at them?" Hardwick asked, convinced that she didn't need to see them to know what they showed because she'd been the one to commit the murders and was therefore all too familiar with what those photographs contained.

"I don't particularly want to look at what I can only presume are gruesome photos of dead bodies, Detective. Unless you want to be cleaning up vomit from your floor."

Wilson glanced at Hardwick concern knitting his brow. This wasn't going according to script.

"The cellphone and SIM card were recovered from the scene," Hardwick lied smoothly, and Bethany knew he was lying. If he expected her to flinch, he'd be waiting a long time. "We're awaiting lab results to see if we can recover any fingerprints." *At least tell me that we aren't going to find any*, he implored wordlessly. When she remained silent, he tried for one final hail Mary pass, "we also found where you tossed your taser. We may not be able to find fingerprints on it, but we will be comparing the burns from each victim to the prongs on the weapon itself."

"Is there anything further that you wish to share related to your investigation, detective? If not, I have errands to run before my daughters get home from school." Bethany stood and headed out of the conference room before either detective could respond.

290

"What were you hoping to gain lying about finding the taser? If she's still in possession of it, she's going to know you were lying."

"And if she isn't, she's going to be worrying sick that we'll actually be able to match the prong burns to the victims. You don't really think she would've driven all the way to north Atlanta to dump a burner phone and not throw away the taser too, do you?"

"So, do you think she'll make another trek out there? See if we actually found the stuff? Should we put another officer on her tail?"

"I don't know if the captain will approve a tail, but maybe he can convince his judge friend to get a search warrant for her house."

"I don't know if he'll go for that."

"He'd better."

"What are you thinking?"

"That we just showed all our cards to a very cool poker player, so if we don't convince a judge that we need a warrant to search her premises and fast, she's going to eliminate any evidence that we may have potentially found. Anything she hadn't thought to get rid of before now, at least. In the meantime, get Harding and Cortez to do a deep dive into her past. Officers put together a preliminary background on all our potential suspects, but if memory serves, nothing about her popped. I want them to try again. Find out about her mom and her husband. Talk to previous neighbors to see if they can shed light in places where facts may still be hidden by shadows. Anything that we can convince a judge to give us a warrant for."

Chapter thirty-one

It took a month of dogged determination, the four detectives working the Seeker of Justice case on their own time, since the captain officially closed the file a day after their interview with Bethany Barnstead.

Witness statements trickled in slowly over those thirty days, agonizing Hardwick with the speed in which the data was compiled. He wanted nothing more than to slam the book on this one, hard. Wanted to take the arrest warrant and wave it in their killer's psychologically twisted face. Instead, he continued adding information to the file, closing it, placing it aside, and working on other homicide cases. "Why is it we can close cases in record numbers, but when a serial case comes across our desk, we're like bumbling idiots?" He snapped.

The three other detectives looked up from their own work and speared Hardwick with an 'I feel ya' look.

"I can answer that, "Harding replied. "Because most of the murders committed are done by idiots who don't care whether there is a camera rolling in their face or not. The rest of them get on social media, after having too many beers, and brag about taking someone out. It's everything we've discussed time and again, bruh."

"Yeah, but some serial killers are a whole other breed, man. Especially super smart ones," Cortez continued. "They ain't right in the head, so getting in there to try to suss out their motivations just leaves us feeling like we've ridden one of them twisty, scary roller coasters at Six Flags."

"That, or they use every tactic they've seen, heard, or read about in order to ensure they foil our attempts at catching them. Those are the ones we have a hard time with," Wilson added. "The intelligent ones who know how to get around our forensic measures. Fortunately, we've captured a few of those too, so our record isn't completely tarnished."

"Yeah, we just couldn't catch the last two to terrorize Atlanta," Hardwick huffed.

"Nothing from neighbors about Miss Barnstead's past?" Harding asked.

"If she was ever abused by her mom or her husband, she never let on that she was," Hardwick admitted. "And the death of her mom just shows as 'accidental death' and her husband shows as 'natural causes'. Nothing to prove otherwise."

"So, nothing denoting that the mom or husband died in the same way as that mentioned in the memoirs of our killer?"

"No, but I'm still keeping that as part of the data to add to our evidence package if we ever collect enough data for a search warrant or arrest warrant. Maybe if we get enough to get a search warrant, we can also move to exhume the bodies to see if there isn't anything that can link causes of death with what the manuscript says. I just wish someone who knew her knew about her relationship with—"

"What about her children?" Wilson asked suddenly.

"What about them?" Cortez asked.

"What's to stop us interviewing them? We don't need their mother's permission to talk to them if they're over eighteen. If anyone would know whether our suspect was abused, it would be her children. Likely they were abused too."

"Son-of-a-bitch, why didn't we think of that sooner!" Hardwick shouted, slamming his palms on his desk.

"Out of sight, out of mind," Harding admitted. "We've never even seen her children, and our focus was trying to put a case together against their mom."

"Well, we're going to meet them now. Wilson, let's go—and let's hope to God one or more are over eighteen."

"Remember when he was a fawning idiot?" Cortez grinned as the two detectives tore out of the office. "Now, he's done turned into a right good detective."

"Who? Wilson or Hardwick?" Harding quipped.

Epilogue

Hardwick, Wilson, Cortez, and Harding stood on the outskirts of the cemetery where the burial service was being held for Bethany Barnstead. Hardwick fought back the tears as his gaze drifted to her four daughters, hugging each other tightly as the casket was beginning to lower into the ground.

"Do you think she knew she was dying and decided to take a few scumbags out with her before she went? Think that's why she did what she did?" Harding asked quietly.

"No, I think that she was horribly abused in ways that we never discovered, and that somehow set her on a path to try to protect others like her. It was a twisted path but with righteous intent, I think," Hardwick answered.

"I wish we could've have gotten some answers from her daughters though," Cortez said. "I think that would have provided us some closure on this case."

"It's pointless now. It would serve nothing but our sense of curiosity at this point to question her daughters and I'm not of a mind to drag them through that particular gutter just to assuage my curiosity."

A day earlier, Hardwick and Wilson had stormed from the precinct, determined to get whatever answers they could from Bethany's daughters, answers about her past and—if they were lucky—to the killings. They didn't know if her four girls were privy to their mother's activities but neither detective thought beyond what to do if they were found to be complicit.

At that moment, they were on a single-minded track to gain answers to questions that Bethany refused to give them. The cars parked out front and along the street should have been the detective's first clue that something was up and only Wilson seemed to get a sense that it probably wasn't the best time to intrude on their family.

"Possibly a birthday party or something. Maybe we should do this tomorrow."

But Hardwick was like a Pitbull with a bone, and he refused to back down, "No, this isn't waiting a single day longer."

As soon as the car rolled to a stop, Hardwick got out of the car and headed to the front door. He knocked and was surprised when a young lady, wearing all black, tears streaming down her cheeks, answered. Without a word, she opened the screen door and invited them inside. Looking back, it was their suits. They looked as if they were meant to be at someone's wake. What they couldn't have fathomed when they left the precinct was that they'd be attending the wake of their prime suspect in a spree killing.

For the next hour, people walked around, hugging, and shaking their hands asking, "how did you know Bethany?" to which they could do no more than shake their heads. Fortunately, this was mistaken for grieving, so they were never pressed on it. Eventually, the two detectives made their way over to the four daughters who sat so close to each other on the couch, it was difficult to see where one person started and another ended. They could've easily been fused together in their grief.

Hardwick squatted in front of them, "we're so sorry for your loss."

The four girls just looked through him, gazes glazed over in pain. He stood and walked over to where Wilson stood, trying not to look like a cop, "Let go," he whispered, and they discreetly exited through the front door.

Today, the four detectives that were determined to take this woman down, stood in silence as her body was lowered into the ground. As the funeral drew to a close, the detectives started to make their way to their cars but were surprised when Bethany's girls moved in their direction.

"You were at our mother's wake yesterday," Katie said, choking back renewed tears.

The detectives nodded.

"You're police officers, aren't you?" Julia asked.

They nodded again.

"How did you know our mother?" Jessica asked, her head cocking to one side, her brow lifted quizzically.

Hardwick had never thought as quickly on his feet as he did at that moment, "Your mother was helping us with our domestic abuse task force."

All the girls' brows knitted in confusion.

"Was it part of her therapy? To aid in the capture of those who abused others like our daddy did to her?" Tanya asked, solemnly.

"Stepdad," Katie snarled and then bowed her head onto Jessica's shoulder as her tears started again. Jessica instinctively wrapped Katie in her embrace.

"That's right," Harding stated, his heart shattering for these young women who would now face an uncertain future on their own.

"May we ask how she died?" Wilson queried as sympathetically as he could muster.

"You didn't know?" Jessica asked, confusion in her tone.

"Know what?" Hardwick pressed gently.

"She had stage four brain cancer," Jessica answered, as the tears began to fall again down her cheek. She sniffled loudly, raising her head in determination not to break down. As the eldest, it was up to her now to provide strength for her younger siblings. She couldn't do that if she was a simpering mess. "The doctor said she had a month to live, tops, but when we came home from school one day, she was um…she'd passed away. She never told y'all about the cancer?"

"I guess she wanted to keep fighting against injustice and feared we'd stop her if we knew," Hardwick answered truthfully, for they truly would have stopped her fight against injustice, if she'd carried on.

Jessica nodded, "that was just like her. We didn't find out until a couple of weeks ago either. She kept it from us too." The girls huddled together as their tears started falling again. The pain and anguish more than the four detectives could bear.

"If you girls need anything, don't hesitate to let anyone of us know, okay?" Cortez offered, passing over one of his cards. The three other detectives did likewise, then fought back tears of their own, when the girls came forward and gave them all a hug.

"Maybe at some point down the road, we can come and help on your task force. I think our mom would like that," Jessica whispered.

"I have no doubt," Hardwick confirmed and then watched them walk away.

Wilson placed his hand on his partner's shoulder, "I think we can satisfactorily close the book on this one, don't you?"

Hardwick nodded and they all turned and made their way back to the precinct, satisfied that the Seeker of Justice had been put to rest.

AUTHOR BIO

Barbara Woster is an author, educator, and business owner. Her passion for books goes all the way back to when she was 14 years old, when her dad gave her a novel by Clive Cussler. On that day, she fell in love with the written word and decided that she, too, wanted to entertain readers across the globe. Although she writes in many genres, her passion lies in suspense. To learn more about her and her work, visit her website at https://BarbaraWosterAuthor.com

Also from this author:

CRIME THRILLERS:
36 Hours (a Detective Hardwick novel)
Killing Faith (international crime)
Edge of Insanity (paranormal crime)

ROMANTIC SUSPENSE:
Desires of a Deceiver
Fate's Intervention
Only One
Whispers of the Heart

TIME TRAVEL:
Love Through Time

HISTORICAL DRAMA:
Dreamer of Destiny
Victim of Love

EARLY READER/MIDDLE GRADE:
Ehtaria: a land of their own
I Am Proud of Who I Am: I hope you are too (15-book series)
The Purple Christmas Tree

NONFICTION:
Parenting in the 21st Century: a horror story

https://BarbaraWosterAuthor.com
Follow on:
Facebook https://facebook.com/BarbaraWosterAuthor
Instagram: https://www.instagram.com/barbarawoster/
X: https://twitter.com/BarbaraWoster